THE FOX'S LAMENT

Barbara,

THE FOX'S LAMENT

And Other Stories

with best wishes

ADRIENNE HOWELL

Adrienne Howell

THE SUNDIAL PRESS

THE FOX'S LAMENT
And Other Stories

First published in 2018
by The Sundial Press

A CIP catalogue record for this book is available from the British Library.

ISBN 978-1-908274-80-9
Printed in England

THE SUNDIAL PRESS
Sundial House, The Sheeplands, Sherborne, Dorset DT9 4BS

www.sundialpress.co.uk

To the memory of Bernard, a constant support,
and my mother, Grace, always an inspiration.

CONTENTS

MIRIAM'S CHILD

Miriam Gray went to church every Sunday although she did not care for the modernised Order of Service. She particularly disliked the Reverend Riddick's cheerful instruction that worshippers give one another 'a sign of peace and friendship'. If she found herself forced to share a pew, Miriam offered a gloved hand and a stiff, upright stance. She wanted none of what her mother had decried as 'happy-clappy stuff' in church. Miriam intended to maintain proper decorum in the House of God.

But on the first Sunday in Advent she was not alone in the pew. Miriam's reluctantly proffered hand was held by a young man. A golden young man. He smiled and gave her the sign of peace. Miriam forgot decorum. She regretted the soft leather gloves chosen to match her Sunday suit. The warmth from his fingers seeped through to her palm. She was suddenly light-headed.

'Are you all right?' The young man steadied Miriam, his arm going about her waist.

'Thank you, yes,' said Miriam. 'Just a little dazzled.'

'Dazzled?'

Miriam blushed.

'Dizzy,' she corrected. 'A little dizzy.'

'Oh!' He pulled a wry face. 'And I thought I'd finally met someone who recognised my dazzling qualities.'

'But I do,' said Miriam. 'You're golden.' She sat, bedazzled, as the rest of the congregation rose to sing the final hymn.

The young man sat with her and held her hand. 'I don't think you're too well. You're very flushed.'

'Flu perhaps,' sniffed Miriam. 'It's going about.'

'I think you should go home.'

'Oh, no.'

'I'm sure God won't mind. It's very cold in here.' And gently but firmly, he guided Miriam out of the pew and down the nave to the west door.

Miriam had dreamt of walking down the aisle of St. Gregory's on the arm of just such a man, but not dressed in navy-blue serge with matching gloves and handbag. Not with a sparse congregation raising their eye-brows and faltering in their singing, nor with the sidesman enquiring,

'Are you all right, Miss Gray?'

'Flu,' she said. 'So sorry.'

'I've never left a service early, not for years,' said Miriam, 'not since I was a child.' She leant on the young man's arm as they walked. The chill winter air had no sobering effect. She was still … dazzled.

'I came over poorly and was sick all over my Sunday shoes. Mother was mortified. Made me apologise to the vicar although she was the church cleaner at the time'

'It wasn't your fault.'

He's so kind, thought Miriam. Kind and beautiful. Fair haired. Blue eyed. He was golden in the grey December light. Miriam felt buoyed up by his presence.

'And I must apologise to Reverend Riddick for today.'

'Do you feel sorry?'

Miriam was excitingly alarmed to realise that she did not feel sorry. She preferred the young man's company to Reverend Riddick's blessing. She was thrilled to have an escort. Since her mother's recent death she was on her own and felt her single status most sharply after church. When the unity of worship was over couples linked arms and set off for lunch; families talked and laughed together, trod the churchyard's gravel path with a common purpose. Miriam went home alone and waited for Monday.

'No, I'm not sorry,' she said. 'Not sorry at all.'

'Nor am I,' said the young man. 'The Reverend Riddick was far from inspiring. I'll give him four out of ten and a 'must-do-better' report to his boss.'

Miriam laughed. She had never felt so relaxed in masculine company.

'What's your name?' she asked as they reached her cottage.

'Tobias.' He held out his hand.

'And I'm Miriam.' She took his hand. 'Do come in for a sherry.' She led the way into her sitting-room.

The sherry was poured, sipped and put aside. Miriam felt drawn by an invisible thread to the golden Tobias. Her lack of experience, normally so inhibiting, did not worry her. Tobias was different. She enjoyed his golden kisses and his golden touch. He was gentle but commanding. As they moved into her bedroom her Sunday suit was discarded, her blouse unbuttoned, her petticoat slipped away. Miriam felt each progression to be pre-ordained. This was meant to be.

'Yes! Yes!' she cried as they fell upon her bed.

Tobias' bright aura enveloped her. She was glowing. Miriam let out an involuntary shout of joy. In that moment she knew who she was – and she knew what Tobias was.

On Monday Miriam decided to tell Janet. She wanted someone to know that she was different and nothing would ever be the same again. Janet, thrice married and divorced, seemed the logical choice. They worked together in the stock room of the county library. Miriam supposed they must be friends.

'Really, Miriam? You finally did it?'

Miriam nodded.

'Oh, I should have guessed.' Janet hugged her. 'You've got that glow.' She stood back and looked at Miriam. 'That special glow.'

'I didn't realise it would show,' said Miriam.

'Love shows,' enthused Janet. 'A woman always looks her best when she's in love. I was positively radiant with each of my fellers, to start with, anyway. What's his name?'

'Tobias.'

'And you and this Toby ...'

'Tobias,' Miriam corrected.

'All right, Miss Prim, you and Tobias ... you honestly, truly, actually slept together, in spite of all you've said about modem morals?'

'This is different,' said Miriam. 'Tobias is an angel.'

'Angelic doesn't last,' sighed Janet. 'Believe me, I know from bitter experience. Men are no angels.'

Surrounded by millions of words, Miriam could find few to articulate her inner certainty.

'But I know he was an angel. I know.'

Such faith was new to her, instinctive not reasoned, a brightness of her soul not her intellect.

'And I'm carrying a child. A special child.'

'Miriam! Steady on! It was only yesterday and well, love, at your age and first time, it would be a small miracle.'

Miriam smiled triumphantly and nodded. 'That's what it is. A miracle.'

'You're mad,' said Janet, taking books from a trolley and edging them onto shelves. 'Menopausal, I shouldn't wonder.'

'I am with child,' insisted Miriam. 'And he's going to change the –'

'One day pregnant,' interrupted Janet with mock admiration, 'and Miriam knows with absolute certainty she's having a boy.'

'Yes,' cried Miriam, 'and he'll put the church back on the right road.'

'Because his father is an angel.'

'Yes,' shouted Miriam, slamming books onto shelves. 'Yes! Yes! Yes!'

'Miriam, love.' Janet moved the trolley out of reach. 'I think you need a cup of tea and a test. I'll nip down to Boots while the kettle boils.'

'Pregnant!' The vicar spluttered, his mouth full of Miriam's sponge cake. 'And is this the cause of your outbursts in church?'

'Yes.' Miriam patted her stomach and sang out, 'He's coming. Alleluia!'

'Miriam!'

'But I thought you'd want to give the church the good news.'

The Reverend Riddick sat silent, stroking his grey goatee into a perfect point, a signal to parishioners that he was communicating with a higher authority on what to say next.

'Miriam …' the vicar clutched at his beard, 'Miriam …'

'Yes?'

'Are you sure? I mean, absolutely certain?'

'From day one and the doctor says I'm three months gone.'

'I never thought this of you, Miriam, I must say. Will you tell me the father's name?

'Tobias.'

'Tobias who?

'He doesn't have a surname. He's an angel.'

The Reverend Riddick tightened the grip on his beard and stared at Miriam. She met his gaze wide-eyed and smiling. For a moment he imagined she was golden. Glowingly golden.

'Angels don't father children,' he said and the moment was lost, dismissed as a trick of the light.

'How do you know?' demanded Miriam. 'They were always around when barren women in the Bible became pregnant. Sarah in the Old Testament, Elizabeth in the New.'

'Miriam, my dear,' the vicar spread his arms wide as if to address a mighty congregation.

'You're in shock. The loss of your mother and now this … er … this difficult situation. But attitudes have changed, you know, being a single mother isn't the shame it once –'

'You don't believe me,' interrupted Miriam quietly.

'Of course I do,' protested Reverend Riddick, 'at least

that you're pregnant, but I believe you're feeling ashamed because you've fallen short of the church's teaching. You're upset that you've let yourself, and your dearly departed mother, down. But there is forgiveness, my child, there's no need to invent stories.'

'You don't believe in angels?'

'Well …' the vicar spoke deliberately, carefully, 'not the sort with wings and halos.'

'Oh, that's good.' Miriam clapped her hands joyfully. 'Tobias didn't have wings or a halo, but I knew he was an angel. He was golden. Didn't you notice that? So golden.'

The Reverend Riddick hurried home to the vicarage planning out a letter to the bishop and making it clear that he had not seen the golden Tobias in his church.

'The woman's a dyed-in-the-wool reactionary and any child likely to be brought up the same,' said the Bishop. 'She must be kept quiet or we'll have a media circus descending on Saint Gregory's.'

'You think so, bishop?' asked Reverend Riddick, who thought a bit of publicity might be just what his Church Repair Fund needed.

'I know so. Imagine the headlines …'

The Reverend Riddick closed his eyes and imagined Miriam, all tweed and pearls, pictured on the front page of the tabloids with the headline, ***Pregnant by an Angel?*** in bold black type.

'And the questions,' continued the bishop. 'Whatever

the church said would be seized upon and used against us. We're in a no-win situation here until the matter is resolved.'

'You mean there's a possibility she's telling the truth?'

'Oh, no, no, dear boy, the church gave up on a second coming long ago.' The bishop sat silent and thoughtful for a moment. 'But,' he leant forward and tweaked the Reverend Riddick's beard, 'we should prepare for all eventualities. Like the wise virgins in Saint Matthew who knew not the day or the hour, we must be watchful so that we are ready and waiting when called upon. Now,' he lowered his voice to a whisper, 'tell me about Miss Gray. Is there someone close to her? A friend, perhaps, who knows her hopes and dreams. Someone we can liaise with?'

The vicar brought Miriam a letter from the bishop. Handwritten and hand delivered to her cottage.

'I'm to take back your answer,' he said. 'Properly signed.'

Miriam tore open the vellum envelope.

The bishop noted her '*most interesting condition*' and suggested that the church provide private facilities for the remaining months of her pregnancy and the confinement.

'He must realise I've been chosen.' Miriam was jubilant.

'There's more,' said Reverend Riddick.

Miriam read on. In return she was to desist from claiming that Tobias was an angel or making any announcements on the advent of a special boy-child.

'But why not? It's true.'

'The bishop is thinking of security. The safety of yourself and, most importantly, that of the child.' The vicar offered Miriam a pen and urged her to sign acceptance. 'Remember King Herod.'

Miriam signed.

'Oh, well done.' The Reverend Riddick whisked away the agreement to which Miriam had penned her neat signature. 'Now we can look after you and keep the baby safe.'

Miriam decided to swear Janet to secrecy.

'You haven't told anyone about me and Tobias, have you?'

'False alarm, was it?' asked Janet.

'Have you?' demanded Miriam.

'Not yet,' said Janet, who did think the tabloids might pay good money for the story when Miriam was more heavily pregnant. 'Why? What's up? Have you lost it?'

'No, he's fine. But I've been stupid. I didn't realise there might be danger.'

Miriam explained the bishop's concern. If the story of Tobias got out, her son could be the target of a multitude of bigots and religious fanatics each claiming him for their own. So the diocese would look after her with Reverend Riddick appointed her spiritual guardian and counsel. In this way the child would be safe and she would be spared the embarrassment of sharing a maternity ward with much younger mothers, who would be visited by proud new fathers and doting grandparents.

'Well, at least the church is taking notice,' said Janet, 'but you'll want a friend with you as a birthing partner. I doubt the bishop will offer to rub your back … and seeing I've had three of my own … and know about Tobias, I think I qualify.'

'Oh, Janet,' Miriam hugged her. 'I'd like you to be there. I'm sure the vicar will agree.'

'Push!' ordered the midwife.

Miriam screamed.

'Push hard!'

Miriam was pale, her breathing urgent and shallow, her arms flailed about seeking the gas and air. Janet put the mask to Miriam's face, 'Not long now, love. Nearly there.' Janet decided Tobias was an impostor or surely Miriam would be having an easier time.

'Sod all these arrangements. She needs to be in hospital. I'll tell vicar.'

'One last push,' demanded the midwife.

'God help me,' wailed Miriam, bearing down in a haze of sweat and blood.

The child was born, scooped up and away by the midwife as Miriam, eyes closed in exhaustion, fell back onto the pillows.

'It's a girl,' said Janet.

Miriam's eyes opened wide and staring.

'You have a lovely baby girl.'

Miriam screamed. A scream of disbelief more anguished than the recent pangs of childbirth. 'No … o … o! Oh, no … o … o!'

A piercing, heart-sick cry of shame and spiritual loss that echoed out into the night and, for a moment, stopped the Reverend Riddick in his tracks.

'Don't you want to see your daughter?' asked Janet attempting to comfort Miriam as the placenta was delivered.

'Never! Never! Never!'

Miriam pushed Janet away, turned her back and sobbed herself to sleep.

Miriam Gray goes to church every Sunday because that is what she has always done. She sits alone, stiff, straight-backed, and refuses to give anyone the sign of peace and friendship. She knows what can happen when proper decorum is not upheld and continually seeks forgiveness. The Reverend Riddick wishes she would stay at home. Miriam's troubled presence reminds him of his bishop's power and the bribe of a better living; reminds him of secret deals made with her colleague and a midwife; reminds him of the night he heard that terrible cry as he carried Miriam's new-born son to the bishop's palace. And how, when he stopped for a moment, he saw the baby boy touched with golden moonlight.

The bishop in his palace is untroubled. He is satisfied he is doing his duty as did the wise virgins in the parable. He is watchful and ready for any eventuality. He receives regular reports from a safe house. Regular reports on the progress of Miriam's child.

THE FOX'S LAMENT

Aunt Polly looked as formidable in her coffin as she had in life. Her arms were folded across her body and her fixed expression gave warning to the angels. There would be no argument at the Pearly Gates about her right of admission. Gracie saw Aunt Polly, dressed in her best grey silk, go striding through with a cursory nod to Saint Peter. And then – then she saw Saint Peter calling her back. She's not wearing a hat, thought Gracie in alarm. Aunt Polly's *Book of Manners* demanded a lady wear a hat on all public occasions.

'Aunt Polly's not wearing a hat,' Gracie whispered against her mother's veiled ear.

'Shhhh!' responded her mother. 'Be a good girl.'

Gracie watched the feather in her mother's hat dipping in gentle acknowledgement as mourners crowded the parlour. Of all the ladies present only Aunt Polly was bare-headed – her auburn curls lying loose upon her shoulders.

'But she's going to church,' persisted Gracie, 'and to heaven.'

Gracie saw Aunt Polly impatient at the heavenly gate. Was she waiting, the child wondered, for her Sunday-best hat? But the angels who gathered about her chanted not of pink ribbons and pearl-headed hat-pins, but of sounding brass and tinkling cymbals.

'Though I speak with the tongues of men and angels, and have not charity, I am become as sounding brass, or a tinkling cymbal.'

Gracie swivelled round to stare at the black-draped mantelpiece. There was a space where Aunt Polly's favourite text had hung in a fancy gilt frame.

'Do as your mother says, girl.' Gracie felt her father's restraining hand on her shoulder.

'Aunt Polly doesn't need a hat now.'

'Not even to go to heaven?'

'No.'

'Then what's she waiting for?'

'It won't be for much longer. Keep still and don't fidget.'

Grace studied the sombre suited, black-robed gathering of friends and relations. They'd come, they intoned as they clasped Uncle George's hand, to pay their last respects. And then they huddled together whispering of 'a great loss' and 'no age to speak of.' Gracie tugged at her father's sleeve.

'Why are they whispering? Aunt Polly said it was rude to whisper.'

'Gracie,' her father's voice took on a warning note, 'show some respect. Remember your Aunt Polly.'

Gracie remembered. She remembered Aunt Polly didn't want whispers. Aunt Polly didn't give a fig for their whispers. She remembered how Aunt Polly had said she'd go cheerfully when she heard the fox's lament and how Uncle George had promised to arrange it. Now Gracie knew why Aunt Polly was lingering at the Pearly Gates. She wasn't waiting for her hat. She was waiting for the lament. The fox's lament.

Gracie wanted to ask Uncle George about the fox. How could it come close to the house in daylight? Men and carriages stood outside to frighten it away. Gracie willed Uncle George to assume his military bearing and order them to move. But Uncle George seemed a smaller, shrunken man. He sat staring at the oaken coffin with its rich red lining and brightly burnished handles.

'Why doesn't Uncle George lament?' Gracie asked climbing onto her mother's lap.

Her mother sighed.

'Can't you see how sad he looks?'

'But he doesn't cry,' said Gracie. 'He doesn't cry like the old fox.'

'Hush now.' Her mother's arms tightened around her. 'Foxes don't cry and neither do men like your Uncle George.'

But foxes did cry. Gracie had heard the old fox cry and so had Aunt Polly. She had been staying with her aunt, keeping her company in the little cottage until, as her mother explained, 'She's got used to being out in the wilds.'

The cottage was not so grand a residence as Aunt Polly's town house, but there was still only one bed to each upstairs room and the sheets were crisp and trimmed with lace. Aunt Polly had come and asked for her to stay. She'd come on a washday, hurrying up the path to the wash-house and calling to her sister, 'I need to borrow your Gracie for a while.'

Gracie was left to sort the laundry while her mother stood talking to Aunt Polly.

'No, I can't come away, copper's coming to the boil. What's all this about?'

'I've left him,' said Aunt Polly.

'You've done what?'

'I've left him,' Aunt Polly said again.

'You can't do that.'

'I'll not live with him a moment longer.'

'Oh, think again,' pleaded Gracie's mother. 'Mind what our Mam always said, "Better to lose an argument than a husband".'

'That's a matter of opinion,' countered Aunt Polly. 'I've neither chick nor child to worry about.'

'But what about your lovely house?'

'What about it?' Aunt Polly was defiant. 'I've rented a little place of my own.'

'Rented a place!' Gracie heard horror in her mother's

voice. 'You've gone too far this time, our Polly, much too far. People will talk.'

'I don't give a fig for their whispers,' said Aunt Polly. 'I've my own place now and I'd like Gracie to keep me company. Say she can come. Just till I get used to being on my own.'

Gracie liked staying with Aunt Polly. She had a room and a bed of her own and at bedtime Aunt Polly brushed her hair and told her stories. Stories that ended with everyone living happily ever after. Here the lightness went from Aunt Polly's voice. She would look down and concentrate on the final brush strokes – ninety-eight, ninety-nine, one hundred.

Then she would say, 'Into bed with you, young lady, and don't forget to say your prayers,' adding, as she bent to kiss her, 'and say one for your Uncle George.'

There was no story the evening they saw the fox – only talk of the wild, red creature that dared come so close to their lives. Aunt Polly saw it first.

'Oh, Gracie,' she called softly, as she went to close the bedroom curtains. 'Look what's in the garden.'

The fox, ears pricked, stood sniffing the air.

'It's an old dog fox,' said Aunt Polly. 'See the white tip on his tail. Isn't he beautiful?'

'Yes,' agreed Gracie, wondering if all creatures with red brown hair were beautiful.

The fox moved on, following the slope of the hedge, merging with and emerging from it into the field beyond.

'He's gone.' said Aunt Polly. 'Home to his little vixen.'

'Will he come back?' asked Gracie.

'Perhaps.' Aunt Polly closed the curtain. 'We'll just have to wait and see.'

But they did not have to wait. Encouraged by scraps of food thrown into the garden, the fox came every evening and brought the little vixen. She was smaller, thinner faced, but with the same thick, russet coat and white underbelly.

'They look well together,' said Aunt Polly. 'A handsome couple.'

'Are they married then?' asked Gracie.

'Oh, I think so. See how he takes care of her.'

The fox stood alert, taking messages from the wind. Watching, guarding while the vixen ate.

'I've heard it said,' Aunt Polly fingered her wedding-ring, 'that for all his faults, the old dog fox is a good and faithful husband.'

The hunt came at the end of summer. The pack hounds first; panting, twitching, panicking around the garden. Gracie clung to Aunt Polly's skirt as the dogs rampaged back and forth. Then suddenly, as if pulled by an invisible string, they broke through the hedge and went baying across the field toward the distant copse. Men on horses followed. Men in blood red coats. Men who doffed their hats to Aunt Polly.

'You should be ashamed,' she cried after them. 'Ashamed! They're all God's creatures.'

That night Gracie heard the dog fox cry. She started up in the night wakened by his long, sobbing howl. The grieving continued unabated until Gracie longed for the crowded comfort of her bed at home. She, too, began to cry. Aunt Polly came hurrying into the room.

'Gracie, don't be frightened. It's stopped now.' She held her close. 'It was just our old fox. He has lost his little vixen and is very sad.'

'Is she dead?' cried Gracie, remembering the wild-eyed, slobbering hounds.

'You mustn't be sad,' said Aunt Polly. 'She will hear the old fox wherever she is.'

'Even if she's in heaven?'

'Especially if she's in heaven,' Aunt Polly reassured her. 'She will hear him cry and know that he loves her.' She slid Gracie beneath the covers and tucked her in. 'Now snuggle down and go back to sleep.'

Next morning, when Gracie came downstairs, Uncle George was there.

'Good morning, young Gracie,' he said briskly.

'Good morning, Uncle George,' she replied and wondered if she should kiss his cheek as she had done in the past. But Uncle George made no move in expectation of an embrace. He took a crumpled handkerchief from his pocket, wiped his eyes and his moustache, cleared his throat and announced:

'End of the holiday, Gracie. I've come to take you home.'

He turned and took Aunt Polly's favourite text from the mantelshelf. 'Come and help me pack up her things.'

'What do you think Gracie and I heard last night, George?' asked Aunt Polly as they sat at breakfast. 'We heard a fox's lament.'

'You heard a fox's lament? Is that right, Gracie?'

'Yes. He was crying for his little vixen and he woke me up.'

'Well, I never!' exclaimed Uncle George, smiling at his wife. 'A fox's lament. That's very rare. Very rare indeed. You must be two extra special ladies.'

'I would hope for such a lament at my passing,' said Aunt Polly, her cheeks flushed pink. 'Then I'd go cheerfully into heaven.'

'Anything you want from now on,' said Uncle George. 'Though I speak with the tongues of men and of angels, and have not charity, I am become as sounding brass, or a tinkling cymbal.'

The black-coated, solemn-faced undertaker stood at the parlour door and the mourners began to bestir themselves. Gracie's mother pushed her toward the coffin.

'Go bid farewell to your Aunt Polly,' she urged. 'You must touch her or she'll come back and haunt your dreams.'

Gracie clung to the edge of the coffin. Her fingers felt the ripple of a fancy frame between the red and the grey silk. The angels began to chant again. She looked at Uncle George. Where was the old dog fox? Why didn't he come?

'Touch,' insisted her mother. 'Put your hand to her cheek.'

Gracie slowly put her hand to Aunt Polly's cold, white cheek but jumped back as Uncle George let forth an animal cry. He threw himself upon the open coffin, his body heaving and racked with sobs. It was the fox's cry of anguish. It was the fox's lament. Gracie began to weep as she saw Aunt Polly go cheerfully through the Pearly Gates.

JIMMY ONE-EAR'S SECRET

'Jimmy One-Ear is coming home.'

The news was shouted from door to door, over garden gates and down the village street.

'Jimmy One-Ear is coming home.'

It reached the pub, the playground, the priest and Mary Ann.

'Jimmy One-Ear is coming home.'

He was coming to visit his mother, to stay in the little cottage where he'd been born and bred.

'Been round the world has my boy,' said his proud mother. 'I've got the postcards to prove it.' She pulled a fistful from her handbag and waved them in the air. 'And now he's coming home.'

The village made plans to welcome back its most famous son. Jimmy One-Ear was a star. Both the critics and audience agreed on that.

'A magic act!'

'Holds you spellbound!'

'Jimmy Molloy is sheer magic!'

The villagers knew better. Jimmy's act was not sheer magic. It was fairy magic.

Jimmy had been born with two ears but somehow, at the age of ten and a bit, he lost one. He went to bed with two ears – one on either side of his face in the normal fashion – but got up for breakfast with only one.

'Without a word of a lie, that's how quick it happened,' declared his mother. 'Sure the thing just disappeared overnight. Withered away, or dropped off, or something, without so much as a whimper out of him. He supped up his porridge and got ready for school as happy as a sandboy. Weren't surprising I never noticed anything at first.'

She noticed the missing ear – or rather the space left by the missing ear – when Jimmy put on his school cap. She'd bought a large size to allow for growth and now the cap fell lop-sided on her son's head for want of even support. Mrs. Molloy was perplexed. Hadn't she washed and scrubbed two ears the night before?

'Did I mangle your ear, son?' she asked, fearing her own strength in the face of a boy's natural resistance to soap and water, particularly about the ears.

'No, Ma,' said Jimmy and went on his way to school while his mother hurried into the scullery to examine the flannel and shake out the towel, just to be certain.

'I've lost me ear, so I have,' Jimmy proclaimed proudly to his classmates in the playground. 'Line up if you want a look. It's one of them mysteries of the universe. Here today. Gone tomorrow. Like me very own daddy. Only me ear was 'ere yesterday and gone today.'

He removed his cap with a showman's flourish. His sweetheart, Mary Ann, first in the line, screamed as loud a girlish scream as she could muster and ran to tell their teacher.

'Please, Miss,' she gasped, 'Jimmy's lost his ear.'

Miss felt her breakfast go heave-ho but she swallowed hard, grabbed the iodine and bandages, and followed Mary Ann into the playground.

'Out of the way all of you,' she ordered. 'Let me look at Jimmy's ear.'

'You can't look at it, Miss,' said Jimmy. 'It's disappeared.'

'Don't be silly, Jimmy.' She grabbed at his cap. 'Let me see.'

The children jigged gleefully up and down and laughed aloud because they knew Jimmy was right and their teacher wrong. All that remained of Jimmy's left ear was a pink plug of skin like a wodge of chewing gum stuck in an ink-well.

'What have you done with your ear?' asked Miss, her bacon and eggs settling again.

'It's a mystery, Miss,' said Jimmy. 'Like your red pencils.'

'Oh, the Little People take them,' volunteered Mary Ann. 'Sure red's their favourite colour next to green.'

'Don't be silly, child,' said the teacher. 'There's no such thing as fairies.'

'Oh, Miss,' chorused the children, aghast. 'What if they hear you, Miss?'

'Be quiet,' snapped Miss. 'Jimmy's had an accident and Doctor Mac has sewn him up.'

Jimmy shook his head which annoyed his teacher, who brooked no answering back or contradiction from her pupils. She sent him home with a note because, she argued, he wasn't completely present.

'Your teacher says I'm to take you to the doctor,' said Mrs. Molloy. 'I was thinking the very same meself only yer ear doesn't seem to bother you none.'

'It doesn't,' said Jimmy. 'How can it bother me if it isn't there?'

'If we were to find it,' suggested his mother, 'if you knew where you'd lost it, perhaps Doctor Mac could sew it back.'

'I don't know where it is,' said Jimmy, a mite too quickly for his mother's liking.

'Well, I'm not having Miss Know-All-There-Is-To-Know-About-Kids look down her spinster nose at me,' she declared, and grabbing Jimmy by his remaining ear, she marched him to the surgery.

'A very tidy job,' said Doctor Mac. 'Very tidy indeed. Such tiny stitches. Barely visible. Did you take him to the hospital yourself?'

'I did not,' protested Mrs. Molloy and explained the overnight sensation.

'Dear me,' said Doctor Mac, 'and did you find the missing member?'

'Not a sign of it,' replied Jimmy's mother, 'tho' I scoured the house from top to bottom.' She wiped a tear from her cheek. 'But I forgot the potato peelings till it was too late. Oh, you don't think the chickens …? I couldn't bear the thought. Not in me best brown eggs.'

'Don't fret, Ma.' Jimmy reassured her. 'Me ear's not anywhere at home.'

'Then where is it?' demanded Mrs. Molloy. 'You had it when you went to bed.'

But Jimmy would say no more however much his mother threatened his remaining lobe.

'There, there,' soothed Doctor Mac. 'No harm done. He can manage just as well with one ear. It's not at all like losing a limb.'

'Is that so?' said Mrs. Molloy. 'Then be so good as to write the same for his teacher. I can't be having him under my feet all day.'

And Jimmy left the surgery clutching a note which stated that he was fully fit for school.

As soon as Jimmy and his mother were out the door, Doctor Mac dialled up Father Floyd.

'Would you be joining me for a drink tonight, Father? I've something I think might interest you.'

The doctor recognised a remarkable recovery when he saw one and the stitching around Jimmy's missing ear was out of this world. Tiny, tiny stitches. No-one could claim those minute sutures were his handiwork.

'Out of this world is right,' said Father Floyd as he sat in Mrs. Molloy's kitchen and inspected the neat knob which now plugged Jimmy's left ear-hole. 'I can barely see the stitches through my magnifying glass.'

'Would it be a miracle then Father?' asked Mrs. Molloy. She crossed herself and then her fingers in the hope that a missing ear might prove more profitable than selling eggs.

' 'Twould be very good for the place, so it would,' said the priest, sending up a silent prayer.

'Be my best boy, now,' urged Jimmy's mother. 'Tell Father Floyd what happened.'

But Jimmy refused to answer. No amount of coaxing, cajoling or hints of future punishment could persuade him, and Father Floyd went home none the wiser.

'Is it can't tell or won't tell,' sobbed Mrs. Molloy, crying into the chicken feed.

'I promised not to tell,' said Jimmy. 'I must never tell.'

His mother left off mashing the chicken meal into boiled potato skins.

'Saints preserve us! Have you been with the Little People?'

'Stop all these questions.' Jimmy put a hand over his one ear. 'I'm not going to listen.'

'Haven't I enough troubles?' His mother raised her voice. 'First yer daddy gone and now yer ear.'

'Oh, don't worry, Ma,' said Jimmy. 'If I keep my promise, it'll be all right.'

It was all right. Better than all right. Miss declared that Jimmy was more in tune with a single ear than he ever had been with two. His hand went up to answer every question she put to the class. He suddenly knew the dates of every reigning monarch and major battle, could recite his tables from two to twenty and scored ten out of ten in spelling tests.

Mary Ann must be whispering in his good ear, thought Miss, and promptly separated the pair.

But Jimmy's progress continued apace. He went from near bottom of the class to the very top and won a coveted place at the Grammar School for Boys.

'A late developer and a rising star,' wrote Miss on Jimmy's end of school report and enclosed ten shillings for his uniform fund.

She was convinced of her own part in Jimmy's success but his classmates were not so certain. Jimmy was keeping his secret and the red marking pencils continued to go missing.

When Jimmy left school he became a star, but not in the manner his teacher had imagined.

'My best pupil,' she wailed. 'A scholarship boy and what does he do? He takes to the stage, so he does.'

'There, there,' comforted Doctor Mac, 'it's not at all like taking to drink. He's making more money than we are.'

Jimmy was the undefeated champion of a radio quiz show. Each week the villagers tuned in their wireless sets to hear Jimmy answer every question correctly, and every answer meant more money. His long running success attracted the attention of a leading London agent who sought Jimmy out and tested his knowledge with the aid of the *Encyclopaedia Brittanica*.

'Right, man,' he said, when he got to Z, 'Here's the deal. The missing ear must go.'

'It's gone already,' said Jimmy, 'but don't ask how.'

'I mean hide it, man. The ladies, bless 'em, won't fall for that lop-sided look. Cover up your missing ear and you'll be a star. Together we'll make it to the top.'

Jimmy shook the agent's hand and signed to grow his hair.

At home he was still Jimmy One-Ear but on theatre billboards be became 'The Amazing Memory Man'. He travelled the world – a walking, talking encyclopaedia. No question posed by an audience, no query – fact or fiction – ever floored Jimmy. The only question he couldn't, or rather wouldn't, answer to those few who noticed was, 'What happened to your ear?'

It wasn't long before Mrs. Molloy gave up keeping hens and bought her eggs from the village shop. Both she and her cottage were prettied and preened and dressed in the best. She was among the first in the parish, along with Doctor Mac and Father Floyd, to boast a new-fangled television receiver.

'I'll invite Miss Know-All-There-Is-To-Know-About-Kids to watch Jimmy's show,' she announced as she selected six eggs over the counter. 'Course, she doesn't know what my boy knows or she'd have a set of her own.'

'He's a clever one to be sure,' agreed the other shoppers.

'Touched,' said Mrs. Molloy. 'But we don't ask by who. 'Tis nae respectful. Don't you agree?'

Indeed they did. The Little People might be listening and anyone with any sense knew that fairy folk guarded their privacy with zeal, and meted out punishments to those who lacked proper respect. Who wanted to find the wrong shopping, or worse, when they got home?

When Jimmy One-Ear came home the flags were flying and the band playing. His former classmates queued to shake his hand and collect his autograph. Mary Ann – first in the line – fluttered her eye-lids and sighed as womanly a sigh as she could muster. Jimmy kissed her cheek and took her off to Father Floyd. They were married by special licence within a month.

'Sure, I think The Little People whisper in that missing ear,' mused Mary Ann on their wedding night.

'Don't ever ask,' said Jimmy, hugging his bride. 'That's my one and only secret.'

WINTER ELM

The old man knew that he was dying. He knew it as surely as he knew which wood to cut from a straggling thorn or which plant to uproot when thinning out. Nature's signs of pervading weakness were ever apparent to those with eyes to see them. And now he recognised those signs, felt them deep within himself.

He told the nurse, told her not to bother overmuch but, Lord, she was a stubborn one.

'I'm not long for this world, missie. You'll see.'

'Nonsense,' she retorted, 'you've just been neglecting yourself, that's all. You should be in hospital, that's where you should be.'

She glanced around the untidy bedroom and endeavoured to bring some order to the heap of bed-clothes under which the old man was lying.

'You'd be far more comfortable in hospital, now wouldn't you?'

The old man knew she meant well but he could be stubborn too.

'I'm comfortable enough. Don't bide and keep on so.'

'It could come to hospital yet,' the nurse continued, 'the doctor will decide.'

She straightened the bed-clothes and tucked them tightly under the mattress as his mother had when he was a child.

'I'll be six foot under afore that day comes,' he muttered rebelliously.

'Now, we don't want to hear talk like that.'

'Why not?' he argued. 'Can't last for ever can I?'

The nurse picked up her bag.

'I' ll look in again tomorrow.'

The old man counted her down the narrow stairs – one, two, three, four.

'Oh, missie,' he called.

The nurse retraced her steps. 'Well?'

'I suppose you'll be telling me next that me great tree's not dying neither.'

The great elm had taken sick several seasons back. The old man had read the signs – the too early touches of autumn colour, branches out of step with season. He urged and chided the tree to contain the blight, but he learnt it had not the power to do so. Kindly neighbours read him learned articles, brought him newspaper cuttings, pictures and maps, all charting the dreadful progress of disease through the lanes and fields of England. He judged then that he and the elm might finish their allotted time together and that seemed fitting. The nurse, however, was not to be outsmarted.

'But you,' she prepared to leave again, 'have not got Dutch Elm disease.'

'Reckon I have, missie,' he said. ' 'Tis winter for both of us. Shan't leave him for none of your hospital, doctor or no doctor.'

When the nurse had gone the old man struggled to free the trapped bedclothes. He was not in some sterile hospital, but in his own room with its smell of damp thatch and tobacco, and he wanted his bed to feel like his bed. The effort tired him and his hands trembled. Nature could not have sent him a more personal herald of approaching death than the ebbing of strength from his hands.

No-one had use for hands like his any more – thickened, scarred and calloused. But once those hands had been shown respect, for in them had been his skill and his craft. His hands had earned him a fair livelihood because they could work the hazel and the thorn to their will, could so exactly sever and stake living wood to provide barriers, wind-breaks, lines of ownership and protection. Hedges.

When the master hedger let it be known that he wanted a lad, the old man's parents had talked together. That was a rare enough occurrence to silence their children. And then his father talked to him, more words in one stretch than had ever passed between them before.

'A hedger's his own man, son. Landlords always want strong hedges. 'Tis bred in 'em. When master's gone you'll be your own man. A good hedger and ditcher be never short of work. What d' you say, son? 'Tis better than scaring crows.'

And he said, 'Yes,' because that was the answer expected of him. He knew he had no real say in his future. That matter would be decided elsewhere.

His mother prepared and groomed him, slicking down his unruly hair with kitchen grease, and his father presented him to the master hedger.

'This here's Jordan, my eldest,' he said, pushing him forward. 'He's strong for his age and a good lad. Eats what's put in front of him and never brought no trouble home.'

And Jordan looked at the ground and shuffled his feet because he didn't know what to say or where to look.

'Give us your hand, young Jordan,' said the master. 'Let's measure thee grip.' And his hand was held and examined.

'Custodian of the great elm, aren't we?' the master enquired.

Jordan nodded. The great elm straddled their cottage boundary and his father was charged with its care.

'And what do you think of him?'

'Oh, 'tis a fine tree, sir,' Jordan replied, truthfully.

'Awesome, lad. Awesome. And a responsibility.' The master put his face close to Jordan's. 'Grew with our place did thic elm. Could tell a few tales he could. Seen the comings and goings of generations.' He paused and then asked softly, 'Does he tell thee anything, young 'un?'

Jordan dropped his voice to a whisper. 'No,' he said, 'but I sometimes tell him my secrets.'

The master smiled and straightened and nodded at Jordan's father. 'I'll take the lad,' he said. And the matter was decided.

He learnt from the master hedger, became skilled in the use of the billhook and the axe. He learnt to force the necessary cutting edge upon his tools, to measure and select wood by glance and with swift strokes to cut and lay down a hedge.

'Shaping the landscape you be, young Jordan,' the master would say, 'and 'tis living matter you work with. Always remember that.' He told and re-told his young apprentice village histories until Jordan could almost see the men who had worked before them and events long past. He became imbued with a sense of responsibility that bound him to his surroundings. He became as solidly rooted as the great elm itself. Brothers who had gone crow-scaring moved away from childhood haunts; sisters married and managed their own homes and families. Jordan remained. He became the master hedger and eventually sole custodian of the great elm.

The old man could see the elm from the low-set window of his bedroom. A skeleton of a tree with bare, brittle branches and flaking bark; its strong hold as a village landmark becoming more tenuous with each day's wind and weather. He had heard talk, mutterings of gossip, that the tree was an eye-sore and should be felled. There was a rumour that it was to be replaced by a sapling, the variety of which had yet to be decided.

The old man determined not to wait upon such events. He had outlived his usefulness in a society where trees were felled by committee and his once carefully tended hedges were mauled by cutting machines. He took to his bed and informed visitors that only when he, the custodian, was dead and gone could they cut down the great elm.

He was vague about the number of years he had cared for the elm. The repetitive rhythm of the seasons had blurred the edges of a long time. But he remembered the tree of his childhood – a silent companion in boyhood games and fantasies; the starting point of expeditions and finishing line of races and feats of endurance. In his youth the elm stood witness to the stumbling dawn and the weary end of each day's work until his body strengthened and grew accustomed to the hours of physical labour and oblivious to the worst of weather. And when he found himself in an alien landscape, where shattered trees stank of smoke and blood and urine, he thought of the beauty of the great elm as other soldiers thought of wives and sweethearts.

He carried with him in the trenches not only a terror of the enemy, but a fear that some catastrophe would befall the elm in his absence. Yet, when they waved him home from war and he found the tree enduring, he experienced a strange resentment. He did not understand his feelings, not then nor since. He felt uneasy in his return to familiar surroundings knowing that he had been changed. And when the reunions and the festivities were over, he turned his face into the bowl of the elm and wept over the horrors he had seen and survived.

Even tears become slower with age, thought the old man, as he wiped the moistness from his eyes with his bedsheet. But there were other memories shared with the elm that remained undimmed and unconsoled. He first saw Amy in church. She knelt proud among the bowed servants from the big house and tossed her golden curls at the admonishments of the vicar. Jordan did not close his eyes in prayer that Sunday and neither did Amy.

The pain of love surprised him. No-one had told him what would happen; no-one judged there was any need. A child of the countryside was expected to keep his eyes open and observe what was natural in its due season. He spoke Amy's name often to the elm hoping to resolve the feelings which told him what he should do, but forbade him from doing so for fear of offending the loved one.

It was Amy who pressed for his answer, leaning her soft body against his and asking, 'Don't you love me then, Jordan?' He held her close and kissed her gently, wonderingly. He was forming words to confess his love when Amy seemed to panic and broke free.

'If you loved me proper you'd show it,' she challenged, while he stood startled and uncomprehending. 'And you'd carve our initials here,' she beat the trunk of the great elm with her small white fist. 'Here, where everybody could see. Everybody would know.'

'Oh, Amy, not there ...' he began to explain, but she saw his hesitation and turned and ran from him.

Jordan cursed himself for frightening her and for the slowness of his tongue. He should have spoken for her and spoken quickly. Now there was only one way he could do so convincingly. He put a cutting edge upon his knife and carefully carved their entwined initials into the rough bark of the elm. Then he went in search of Amy.

'You've missed her. She's gone.'

'Gone?' Jordan echoed the maid who answered his knock at the big house.

'Well, sent away more like.'

'Sent away?'

'Ah, Amy weren't suitable.'

The girl's words conveyed a criticism that Jordan did not understand.

'You know how it is with some girls,' she added, but it was evident that he did not. 'Amy were pregnant,' the maid said slowly and deliberately. 'Four months gone. Must have known it afore she came. That's what upset the mistress and I can't say I blame her.'

Jordan did not blame Amy. He had put aside his duty as custodian of the elm and had paid the price. He vowed never to do so again.

The old man looked out at the elm – a winter tree in a summer landscape – and knew that his vow was at an end.

'You'm only fit for coffin wood,' he shouted. 'Just like meself.'

THE PRICE OF SILK

I can tell at a glance if a garment is pure silk. Hangs so beautifully does silk. There's nothing can beat it, especially for underwear. Mother taught me that.

'Silk can make a world of difference to a cheap dress, Deirdre-Anne. What's underneath is more important than what Joe Public sees.'

I am always Deirdre-Anne. Double-barrelled like a proper little lady. And Anne with an 'e'. Mother is most particular about that. She is even more particular about her underwear. The box of wild-rose, pale blue, peach and pearly white silk she keeps under her bed.

'Silk underwear does something special. It works its magic on any garment. You remember that, my girl. Never skimp on your undies.' She smooths her hands over her body feeling the sheen of her petticoat, pressing it close to her skin, liking its touch. 'Silk makes you look good and feel good. Silk is class whatever you do.'

And she smiles that strange smile. Not a happy, hello-little-daughter sort of smile, but a sad inward one to herself. A private joke she doesn't share with me. I share jokes with Nanny Gann who lives next door.

Nanny Gann isn't beautiful like my mother. She is big and broad and slow. Her face and hands are all blotched red, but she is warm and loving and always there. She isn't really my Nan but she hugs me to her greasy apron and calls me 'a poor, wee, fatherless mite.' Mother is cross when I ask her what it means.

'You won't be poor, Deirdre-Anne, I'm making sure of that. And go ask Nanny Gann if any of her kids had pretty dresses and black patent shoes bought spanking new.' I sense the question is not meant for Nanny Gann.

I know Mother works hard to give me nice things but this means that on most days our lives touch only briefly as she gets ready to go to work. In the morning she dons the free issue overall and her long blonde hair is tidied into a deftly knotted headscarf.

'Factory hooter's gone, Deirdre-Anne. Take yourself and your toast to Nanny Gann.'

And off I go through the gap in the fence for Nanny Gann to see me to and from school, or keep an eye on me during the holidays. In the evening, after we've had tea, Mother swaps the factory brown drabness for hand-laundered silk and scent.

'Get the box from under my bed, Deirdre-Anne,' she calls from the scullery.

I lie on my tummy and wiggle it from its hiding place.

No ordinary plain box, but a box from Mother's hidden past. A box once fit for a lady's ball gown. Buff brown and patterned with autumn leaves swirling and twirling just as, I imagine, my mother did in the arms of her dance partner. The light picks out a hint of gold lettering.

'Can I open it?'

'Yes, but don't touch. I don't want any little paw marks.'

I lift the lid and rustle away the tissue paper. Which silk will she wear tonight? Wild-rose, pale blue, peach or pearly white?

'Eenie, meenie, miney, mo …'

'Don't touch', says Mother, coming into her room.

She smells of lemons and has let her hair down. She's wearing pale pink panties and I know it will be the turn of the wild-rose petticoat. As always, she sits on the bed and checks it over.

She makes sure no hem stitch has come loose and tests the shoulder straps with a little tug front and back.

'Remember, Deirdre-Anne, a lady's underwear has to be perfect.'

'Why?'

'Well, it's just the way things are.'

'But who's going to see?'

'Oh, hush up, child. Doesn't matter who sees, it's one of the rules.'

'What rules?' I ask.

'The proper people's rules. The rules for ladies and

gentlemen.' She is satisfied the wild-rose is perfect and stands to stretch her slim body as she slips it on. 'Oh, suppose … just suppose I had an accident, got run over by a bus or something, a doctor would see … doctors are gentlemen and gentlemen … well …' She smiles, runs her hands over the sheen of the wild-rose and straightens the lace trim. 'The state of your underwear is as good as a reference, Deirdre-Anne. Now, get yourself off to bed or I'll be late.'

I do as I'm told. There is no hooter for this job and she's always edgy about being late.

Mother comes to tuck me in. She still has to finish dressing and put on her lipstick, but she looks perfectly lovely in her petticoat.

'Snuggle down and go to sleep.' She bends to give me a brief kiss and I feel the cool touch of silk. Tonight wild-rose is my favourite colour, tomorrow it may be pale blue, peach or pearly white. 'Just call for Nanny Gann if you need anything.'

I lie awake that night worrying about her being hit by a bus. I imagine my band-box smart mother lying in some dirty gutter, the pink silk stained with blood, and the doctor, realising she is a lady, putting it to soak in cold salt water. I knock on the wall.

'Goodnight, Nanny Gann.'

The thin partition echoes as Nanny Gann knocks a comforting reply.

I leave school at fourteen because I'm offered a job. I'm to be an assistant in the lingerie department at Harvey's, the smartest and most expensive shop in town. It's the job I've always dreamt of since Nanny Gann and I went window shopping there and I saw Mother's newest soft mauve petticoat and matching cami-knickers on display. I wanted to go inside and touch all the lovely, lacy things, but Nanny Gann hurried me away. Now I am Harvey's newest trainee issued with a smart black uniform and three sets of detachable white collars and cuffs.

I'm ready for my first day at work. Nanny Gann wishes me well but Mother is not so pleased.

'You didn't have to leave school, Deirdre-Anne.'

'I want this job, Mother. I want to work with lingerie, with silk.'

'I would have seen you through college.'

'But you work too hard now. Nanny Gann says you're burning the candle at both ends –'

'Nanny Gann should keep her opinions to herself.'

'– And you should be sleeping in your bed at night.'

'Where does she think I sleep then, when the club closes? What has that old gossip said to you? Has she put you off going to college?'

'No, Mother.' I take her hand. 'It was my decision. With me working you won't have to do two jobs. We can spend more time together.'

She squeezes my hand and sighs.

'I'll keep both going a little longer – just in case you change your mind. Now, fetch out my petticoats, there's a good girl, and don't touch. Silk is for real grown-ups.'

But on my first day at Harvey's I am grown-up enough to hold a silk slip. My supervisor sniffs at the word petticoat.

'Fish wives and factory girls wear petticoats.'

I don't care what she calls it. I am touching silk. My supervisor expects me to be overawed.

'I don't suppose you've seen such beautiful underwear before, Miss Clifford. The material is silk.'

'Yes, Ma'am.'

'Pure silk in Eau de Nil with hand stitched decoration. It must be handled with care. Extra care.'

'Yes, Ma'am.'

I don't let on that I recognise silk, or that I know how to fold the garment. I've seen Mother do it hundreds of times. I watch my supervisor demonstrate the Harvey box packing technique and then she checks my finger nails.

'Keep them short like that, Miss Clifford. It's so easy to snag a delicate garment and any damage is deducted from your wages.' She unpacks the box. 'Now you try.'

The Eau de Nil is packed in the store's own tissue paper, wispy thin sheets of the purest white with a swirly capital 'H' lightly etched all over, like letters traced in snow. My supervisor keeps a steely eye on me. I place the front of the garment down on the tissue, turn the side seams into the back, the hem up to the waist then bring the bodice back over and straighten the seams. The only novelty is the tissue paper that I must crumple and tuck inside the cups so that the front decoration shows up nicely on opening the box.

'Well done, Miss Clifford.' My supervisor claps her hands politely. 'You will assist me on the counter tomorrow morning. Our early customers are often the gentlemen.'

'You mean like a doctor?' I ask.

'Not just doctors. All the customers here are ladies and gentlemen and they must be addressed as "Sir" or "Madam" whether they deserve the title or not. Do you understand, Miss Clifford?'

I shake my head and she explains.

'Gentlemen come to Harvey's lingerie to buy those special gifts for the ladies in their life. Presents for madam, and madam may be his wife or daughter … or …' she wrinkles her nose, 'or very often a lady friend who is exactly the opposite. She is not a lady at all, except at our counter because it pays Harvey's to exercise such discretion. Here both the wife and the courtesan are madam.'

'Courtesan?' I query.

'A polite word,' she screws up her face as though a

foul stench is seeping from under the counter, 'for a woman who sells her favours. A whore who thinks she has class because her clients are gentry and very rich.'

I feel myself blushing.

'A lot of secrets become known to the lingerie department, Miss Clifford. Intimate gifts speak of close and intimate relationships but,' she wags a warning finger at me, 'assistants here keep those secrets and tell no tales if they wish to keep their job.'

'I understand, Ma'am,' I say and nod as wisely as I know how.

The next morning I stand behind the brightly burnished mahogany counter. It has a brass measure inset along its length. My supervisor also has a tape-measure to hand.

'The correct fit is everything, Miss Clifford, as you will learn.'

There are drawers full of silk arranged in threes beneath the counter. Each Goldilock tier contains one colour in a variety of pastel hues and tints.

'Nothing is more unseemly than scrabbling through a drawer for a requested colour,' says my supervisor explaining how the stock is stored.

No 'eenney, meenie, miney, mo' at Harvey's.

The first customer of the day is, as predicted, a gentleman. My supervisor is smiling, anxious to please, whispering discreet questions, nodding at the answers, proffering samples and offering advice until a choice is made.

'Thank you, sir. A beautiful shade. Madam will be delighted. My assistant will pack it for you.' She turns to me, her face unsmiling, and silently mouths the word, 'Courtesan'.

Blush Pink is the lightest of the soft pinks and I am charged with packing it while Sir rests on a chaise longue perusing *The Times.* As I fold the garment into the embossed box, I run my hands lightly over the side seams. I feel the sheen. I like the touch of silk. I close the lid and take the box to the counter. My supervisor rings up the sale on the till. The pounds, shillings and pence leap up. Big, bold, black numbers glaring at me. Staring me in the face is the value of Mother's box of silk. How can she afford it? Her voice echoes in my head,

'You won't be poor, Deidre-Anne, I'm making sure of that.'

And now I know the price of silk.

CATALYST

A barrow. That's how I started in business. On me demob from the Navy I had a barrow down Pompey market. Now look at me – a retail tycoon with loads of dosh and lashings of respect. Mind, no-one's thought to ask how I got that barrow in the first place. And would I tell them if they did? No, I think not. I'd invent another catalyst.

See, I funded that barrow with cash I got from flogging Navy fags. Duty Frees. Blue liners. But if it hadn't been for the ship's cat, there'd have been no barrow. Things would have been different. Very different. That dear old moggy has my undying gratitude and, what's more, Tigger didn't fret that his heroics were kept secret.

I can see that cat now. Belonged to one of the officers and that animal knew it had class. Stalked about the decks; tail up, back arched, whiskers bristling, superior sort of look on his face. I'd never seen a cat quite like Tigger. Sort of brindle, more of a greyhound's markings and, fortunately for me, he could move a bit sharpish as well.

Tigger wasn't exactly yer friendly, cuddly type of cat, but he took a shine to Toby, my oppo on our mess deck. Toby was a country lad from some remote village on Salisbury Plain and he had a way with animals. He could handle that fiery cat.

Toby didn't take kindly to me wanting to put Tigger in the suitcase.

'You can't do that, Fred,' he says. 'It's cruelty to dumb animals.'

'This is an emergency,' I argue. 'It's him or me. Won't be for long.'

Give Toby his due, he went along with me plan.

I was at me wit's end when I saw Tigger prowling about our deck. The idea just popped into me head. As a plan it wasn't fool-proof, but it was the only one I had and I reckoned it was worth a try. If it had gone wrong then, like I said, my life would have taken quite a different turn. I'd have ended up a sorry heap in some alley off Queen Street or done time in the glasshouse on Whale Island, depending on who got to me first.

Toby went all righteous when I told him what I was doing.

'You're a spiv,' he says. 'Running black market fags.'

'You're looking at it all wrong, Toby mate,' I answers. 'I'm helping the war effort.'

'How d'you make that out?' he asks.

'I'm helping those poor sods in factories who'd much

rather be fighting Hitler, and all them lonely wives back home coping with hordes of kids. They can't afford the number of fags they needs to keep 'em from going doolally in this ruddy war.'

I didn't have the guts to ask me contact if he sold the duty frees cheap. I suspect not, but I had me own price and stuck to it. While we were at sea I'd buy up as many fags as I could wangle and flog 'em off when I got back to Pompey. Had to smuggle 'em past the dockyard police, of course, but there were ways and means.

Things were ticking over nicely when me contact – now, he was a spiv if ever there was one – he wanted a big, big order. Offered me the wherewithal to bulk buy, something to stow the fags in and the promise of a bonus.

'Is it a deal?' he asks and shoves this battered brown case in me hand.

'Can but try,' I says and grabs the wad of fivers he's waving under me nose.

Well, to cut a long story short, I got the fags. When we docked I had everything ready to go. Then came the bombshell. There was a crackdown on the dockyard gate. Everyone was being searched. Everyone. No exceptions.

'What are you going to do, Fred?' Toby kept eyeing the case. 'You'll never get that lot through.'

'Got to,' I says. 'I've spent the bloke's money.'

Toby was a good mate. He offered to meet the contact

and tell him I'd been captured, wounded, fallen overboard, anything. I was racking me brains – I wouldn't have sent me worst enemy, apart from Mr. Herr Hitler, to meet that thug with an empty case and a bare wallet – and that was when I had me Tigger moment.

'Get hold that flipping cat,' I says.

Toby looked at me like I'd gone mad 'cos I was emptying the fags out the case and stuffing them out of sight in me kit-bag.

'Get Tigger,' I shouts – and he does.

In spite of Toby's protests I put Tigger in the case and shut the lid. He screeched and scratched for a bit and then lay quiet.

'Not for long, Tigger, old shipmate,' I says. 'I'm relying on you.'

And off I went in the hope of salvaging that bonus.

A big, burly police sergeant stopped me at the gate.

'What you got in the case?' he demands.

I was ready and, fingers crossed, I hoped Tigger was.

'Ship's cat going to the vet, sir.'

'Open up!'

'But sir,' I whine, 'he's a devil to catch and he's quiet now.'

'Open up!'

Down went the case, facing the sergeant as regulations demanded. I clicked it open pulling the lid back towards me. Out flew Tigger like a greyhound from the traps, hissing and spitting mad, clawing the air and catching the sergeant's hand as he jumped back cursing aloud. Talk about a caterwaul!

'Thanks, Sarge,' I says accusing like. 'Now I've got to catch him all over again.'

I grabbed the case and started after Tigger but once out of sergeant's sight, I was back to the ship and up the gangway. Toby helped me re-pack the fags and then went to look for Tigger. I returned to face that sergeant on the gate.

'Ship's cat going to the vet, sir.'

'I hope it's bleedin' terminal'. He waves me through with a bandaged hand.

I walked out them gates real slow and carrying the case so careful, like there was a poorly animal inside. Then round the corner I took to me heels and high-tailed it to Queen Street and that bonus.

Tigger's story might spoil a tycoon's profile so I keep schtum. I don't let on to all and sundry, but I'll never forget him. I can still see that classy cat. Tail up. Back arched. He's right here. On me desk, over the door, on the headed paper and the price-tags. He's the logo for me business – The Tigger Trading Company.

A CRUTCH CALLED ARNIE ARNOLD

Mam meets me from school like always but she's not wearing her old brown coat. She's all dressed up in her Sunday best. Her hair's unpinned and her lips are bright red.

'Are we going somewhere?' I ask.

'No. We're off home.' She takes my hand. 'It's a surprise.'

The surprise is leaning against the kitchen table.

'Say hello to your daddy.' Mam pushes me forward.

'Colin,' says the surprise, 'Colin, me own sweet boy, don't you be feeling awkward now 'cos yer daddy has a crutch.'

Crutch is a word that's new to me and so is this daddy. He doesn't quite match the photo-daddy I've been kissing goodnight while Mam were whispering for God to save him from, 'Them chinky bastards'. This daddy's not that strong, smiling soldier; he's pale and thin and his gun's made of wood.

'This ain't a weapon, son,' he says. 'This, Colin, is a

crutch. It's going to help yer daddy get back on his feet.' And he tucks the black padded end under his arm and hippity-hops around the kitchen.

Mam and I laugh as he topples into the fireside chair.

'Just you wait,' he waves the crutch at us, 'this will be a better friend than a rifle.'

'You'll soon be on yer feet.' Mam gives him tea and a double helping of sponge cake. 'And we'll be dancing down the Palais again.'

'I don't think so, sweetheart. I'm stuck with this thing now.' He strokes the crutch like it's our pet rabbit or next-door's cat. 'It ought to have a name, don't you think?'

'No!' cries Mam.

But he looks to me. 'What shall we call it, Colin?'

'Arnie Arnold,' I shout.

It's a good name because Arnie sits next to me in school and he's called first for everything – same as Colin Young is always last.

'Righty ho!' Daddy pulls a serious face and talks posh. 'Blessed crutch, I baptise thee Arnie Arnold.' And he pours his tea over it from top to bottom.

I'm jumping about all excited, but Mam is on her knees.

'For God's sake, Jack! Look at the mess.'

'Oh, give over, woman. It's just a bit of fun. I want for our boy to be comfortable around this thing.'

'And what about me?' Mam mops up the spilt tea.

'Think I'm comfortable clearing up behind a ruddy crutch?' She wrings out the floor cloth and dirty tea drizzles into the sink.

'Sorry, sweetheart. I weren't thinking. I need to be house trained again.'

'Fat lot of good me trying to teach our boy proper manners.' Mam is busy at the sink directing tea-leaves down the drain. 'It hasn't been easy on me own … not knowing if … if …' She stops to fuss over a splash of water on her dress.

'Colin,' Daddy hoists himself from the chair and tucks Arnie under his arm. 'Go play in the yard.'

But I don't want to play in the yard.

'Don't you defy me, boy.' Daddy comes hippity-hopping toward me. 'Don't you dare! In the yard! Right now!'

I'm sure he wishes Arnie were a real gun. I'm too scared to move.

'Jack!' Mam calls from the sink and gathers me to her. 'Give him time for God's sake.'

'A boy obeys his father anytime.'

'Of course, but he's too young to remember that; he'd barely started school when you were posted. He has to get used to having a daddy again. He needs to get to know you, Jack, not some stupid crutch.'

'Arnie Arnold,' I shout and they both laugh.

'Colin,' says Mam softly, 'do as Daddy says and play in the yard.'

'Arnie and I will be along soon,' he adds.

I slope off to the yard. I feed our rabbit and kick me football against the wall. After a bit, I edge to the kitchen window and peeps in. There's Mam and Daddy – arms round each other and Arnie – swaying on the spot like they're trying to dance. They don't see me. I'm left outside.

I wait and wait and wait in the yard until Mam calls me for bed.

'Kiss Daddy goodnight like always.'

But it's not like always. This is downstairs and the real daddy holds me so tight I feel his shirt buttons pressing hard against my skin.

'You and Arnie didn't come and play,' I mumble against his stubbly chin.

'No. Sorry, son. Overdid it a bit, I'm afraid.'

'Dancing!'

He shoves me away so fiercely I almost fall.

'Spying on me, eh?' His voice is loud and harsh. 'I've had quite enough of that, thank you. You'd best be up them stairs before you get what spies deserve.'

I don't need telling twice. For once I'm glad it's bedtime.

Mam is quiet as she helps me get ready for bed. I remember to brush my teeth without being told.

'All done.' I smile proudly.

'Colin,' she crouches down beside me, 'you are happy that we've got Daddy home, aren't you?'

'I suppose so,' I fib with fingers crossed. 'Where's he been?'

'I told you. Daddy was sent to fight a war in Korea … your teacher showed it you on the big map, don't you remember?'

'Yes! And then he got captured by them …'

'The enemy.' Mam says quickly. 'They put Daddy in a horrid prison camp and he got very ill. But he's home now and we must help him get better.'

'How?'

She walks me into the spare room with the narrow little bed and no space to play.

'By being a big, brave boy who sleeps on his own.' She tucks me in and kisses me goodnight. 'We won't let on you slept in Daddy's bed. It's our secret.'

I don't feel very brave on me own. The sheets are cold and I miss cuddling up to Mam. Then I hear her and Daddy coming up the stairs.

'I can manage,' he insists. 'You go and check on Colin.'

I squeeze me eyes tight shut.

'He's well away,' she whispers.

I hear the door of the big bedroom close and then strange noises. I don't know if Mam is laughing or crying. But I do know that Daddy and Arnie Arnold are with her and I'm not.

I get used to sleeping alone, but not to having a daddy at home in spite of all them that pats me on the head and says how happy I must be.

'Of course he is,' says Mam. 'And so am I.'

But it's her 'let's pretend' voice and I know she's fibbing. Daddy is a puzzle. Mam tells him he's come home with a piece missing and can she have her old Jack back.

'You've got to put it behind you,' she pleads.

And sometimes he does but not for long. He's soon back calling the neighbours spies, or lashing out if I don't eat every bit of me dinner.

'You finish that up, you spoilt brat, or I'll teach you what it means to be hungry.'

Then there's his bag – his work bag which he hides away in the yard shed.

'Don't none of you go nosing in my bag or I'll give you what for.'

Daddy keeps the shed locked and the key in his pocket.

'What's so precious about that old army haversack?' laughs Mam.

'It's mine.' Daddy thumps the floor with Arnie. 'Mine! Mine! Mine!'

'All right, Jack.' Mam's laughter is gone. 'We've got the message.'

Daddy has a new job but he won't say what, or where, except that it's well away from nosey-parker neighbours. And he works funny hours.

'I'm out the army now. I can come and go as I please.'

'Bosses won't stand that for too long,' says Mam.

'I'm me own boss now.'

'Yer own boss?' Mam stops beating up the cake we're making for Sunday tea. 'First I've heard about it.'

'Don't concern you so long as the housekeeping's paid of a Saturday.' Daddy piles coins from his pocket onto the table. 'You're lucky I don't spend it down the pub, like some.'

'I were concerned enough to keep this place going.' Mam starts on the cake again. The wooden spoon I like to lick batters against the mixing-bowl. 'I made sure you had something to come home to. Now I can't be told nothing.'

'Better that way.'

'No it's not. Jack. I'm yer wife and this is not a P.O.W. camp.'

'Then stop the damn interrogating.' Daddy leans heavily on Arnie. 'And leave me be.' He hippity-hops away to the yard.

Mam scrapes the cake mix into a tin and slams it in the oven.

'You go find yer father,' she points to the back door with the unlicked spoon, 'and you tell him I'm off down the Palais tonight.'

And that's our Saturday nights for now – Mam goes

dancing and leaves me with Daddy. Mam is happier, and me and Daddy get on better. We play goalie in the yard, City against United. I always get top score because he has Arnie and can't run.

'I ought to have an Arnie,' I suggest, 'to make it fair.'

'Yer Mam would throw a fit. She don't understand about Arnie.' He bats the ball back to me. 'We'll beat you next week.'

But when Saturday comes there is no football. Daddy is late home.

'Where the hell is he?' Mam puts her ear to the mantelpiece clock. 'He knows it's me night out.'

She has supper on the table, kettle on the hob and a wrap-round pinny over her dance dress.

'You come and have yours, Colin. He'll just have to see to himself.' And she's off upstairs to put on her make-up.

I'm in my jim-jams watching at the window and Mam is sat with her coat on when I see Daddy come in the back gate. He's in a big, big hurry because he comes straight across the yard and doesn't go to the shed first. Mam is on her feet.

'What the hell time do you call this?'

'Sorry, sweetheart, I missed the usual bus.'

'And I've missed me lift.' Mam picks up her handbag. 'But I'm going anyway and you can cough up the fare.'

'No problem.' Daddy is excited and smiling. 'I can

stand you a treat tonight.' He opens the haversack still slung across his chest. 'I've had such a good day. Crowds about. It were worth hanging on for the late pickings.'

'Pickings, Jack?' Mam stares at him. 'That's a funny word to use.' She makes a sudden grab and yanks at the haversack. 'Just what have you got in there?'

Daddy tries to dodge away but Mam is too quick. She pulls so hard on the shoulder strap that Daddy lets go Arnie and topples over. He lies on the kitchen floor, the secret of his work-bag spilled around him: pennies, half-pennies, tanners, shillings, half-crowns – real money, not like the toy stuff at school – there's even a ten bob note.

'My God, Jack!' Mam sinks back on her chair. 'How could you?' She's hugging herself like she's been punched in the belly-button. 'How could you?'

Daddy is on his knees scrabbling up the coins.

'Well, now you know.' He throws a piece of cardboard at her.

There's writing on it. I see a word I know. It's 'Korea' like on our classroom map. Mam hurls the cardboard back and picks up the ten bob note. I try to help Daddy up, but he waves me away.

'You go off to bed, son. Yer mam's going dancing.'

Next morning Daddy is cooking breakfast.

'Where's Mam?' I ask.

He doesn't answer, just plonks a plate of fried bread and egg on the table.

'Eat that up. There'll be no roast dinner today.'

'Why not?'

'Yer mam's gone … gone … visiting.'

Then he just crumples up and is bawling like next door's baby. Tears run down his face and he's babbling words that come so fast I can hardly keep up: filthy huts, rats, sadistic guards, torture, brain-washing, weevils, dysentery, starvation, burning feet …

'Them chinky bastards burnt yer feet?' I grab at words I do understand. 'With matches?'

Daddy manages a thin smile and wipes his eyes.

'No, son, not with matches. Some of us were in such a bad way we got very ill. Our feet felt like they was on fire. It were sheer agony to put a foot to the ground.'

'That's why you have Arnie.'

'I can't rid me mind of the sensation, like I can't be working to order no more. Why couldn't yer mam understand that? I understood about her dancing. I didn't mind one bit. Not one bit. We all need a crutch of some sort.' He's crying again and now I'm afraid.

'Where's Mam?' I whimper. 'When's she coming home?'

Daddy draws me onto his lap and holds me tight.

'I don't know, son. I wish I did. But we'll manage somehow. We'll be on the same team till she gets back. I'll make you that Arnie Arnold you wanted and we'll go hippity-hop together.'

A PROPER JOB

Faces round the wall. Made-up faces. Faces in grease-paint, highlight and shadow. Duncan knew these faces. Knew every inch of them. He'd counted the number of pencilled lines and measured the length of each painted scar. And he spoke to the faces. Addressed kings and commoners by name.

'Wet out today, Othello, old chap. Not that anything can put a damper on your hot temper.'

Famed faces. Framed faces. Made-up faces of made up people. People conceived in solitary state. Purely begot with the sweat of the brow. Created beings claiming more than three score years and ten. Men and women plucked from the air who spoke, proclaimed, held forth for hundreds of years. Duncan knew them all. He knew them well enough to give advice.

'Now what d'you have to go and do a thing like that for? You should have more sense. Use yer loaf for God's sake.'

He'd tell them straight out. Offend or please. Now Othello was playing centre stage and Duncan had taken him to task.

'You listen to me. Forget that Iago chap. Where's yer trust. A marriage should have trust. If I had a woman like your Dessie, I'd hang on to her. I'd hang on for dear life.'

But Duncan did not have a woman like Desdemona. He had Shirley. And Shirley was slowly driving him mad.

'Duncan,' she'd whine, 'Duncan, give up this writing lark and get a proper job.'

That was her constant whinge. Proper job. Proper job. Like the recurring comment of a Greek chorus. Hey, that's not a bad idea, thought Duncan. Thanks, Shirl, I'll put a chorus in my play:

Proper job. Nine to Five.

Proper job. Shirt and tie.

Proper job. Time together.

Duncan took to locking the door of the spare room when writing. Shirley took to beating the paint from its panels with her small, bony fists.

'Duncan! Open this door. We've got to talk.'

He wrote while Shirley's tattoo drummed on insistent. On and on she went in answer to the chorus.

Proper job.

'Open this door, damn you!'

Nine to Five.

'I've been to work all day. I'm your wife not your skivvy. You're a lazy sod, Duncan. A lazy sod!'

He sat at his makeshift desk stealing Shirley's angry words – committing them to paper.

'You hear me, Duncan? Open this door.'

Proper job. Time together.

'You've got ten seconds. Ten seconds! Open this door or I'm leaving. I mean it, Duncan. I'm going and I won't be coming back.'

He opened the door.

'Wake Duncan with thy knocking!'

'You weren't asleep,' snapped Shirley. 'You're up here wasting time and paper. Just look at this room.' She began to collect the crumpled litter of false starts, wrong turnings and discarded sub-plots. Duncan hastily provided a cardboard box and assisted in the clear up.

'I'll see to this.' He gathered up the offending material. Shirley had not acknowledged the Bard's words but she might well recognise her own and Duncan did not want that to happen. Not yet. 'I've told you, Shirl. I'll keep this room tidy.'

'My tidy and your tidy are two different things,' said Shirley. 'There's dust an inch thick under this bed.'

'Bugger the dust,' shouted Duncan. 'What d'you want, Shirl? I'm working on my play.'

It was another bad line. A line that couldn't be consigned to the litter bin.

And Shirley was right on cue. She had rehearsed her list of wants:

Proper job. Nine to five. Shirt and tie.

Proper job. Money in the bank. Deposit on a house. Nice neighbours. Nice garden, lawn and flowers.

Proper job. Proper marriage. Husband and baby.

'I'm fed up,' she finally wailed. 'I never see you. It's scribble, scribble all day and off to that dratted theatre at night.'

'There, there,' soothed Duncan. 'I'll try and get home early tonight.'

'Promise?'

'I promise.' He ushered her out and re-locked the door.

Duncan always made amends to Shirley when she threatened to leave him.

Her desertion was unthinkable while he was nurturing the play. Its shape had to be controlled, well made. The crisis and denouement held back. Shirley couldn't leave until the final act. So he kept his promise and made love to her. Dutifully. Perfunctorily. He reserved passion and power, pressure and pace for the Dramatis Personae of his masterpiece. In the real situation he tended to panic.

'You are still taking the pill?'

'Of course,' said Shirley. 'We couldn't bring up a baby in this place.'

Duncan rolled away from Shirley's relaxed body and lay silent memorizing her response. He felt he owed her a kind word for yet another line of dialogue.

'When the play makes the West End,' he said, 'we'll be able to afford our own place.'

'With a garden,' said Shirley dreamily.

'Of course with a garden, but you'll have to see to it. I'll be writing a follow-up.'

'A follow-up!' Shirley sat up in bed. 'You haven't finished this one yet and you need at least two acts to get in the West End.'

'I know that, Shirl. And I'll have three acts. You'll see.'

'But I don't see. I don't see anything you're doing. I don't even know what this sodding play's about.'

'Well ... it's ... it's about ordinary people,' he hedged, 'like you and me. Folk living plain, ordinary lives.'

'Duncan! People don't want to see ordinary lives in the West End. They can watch telly for that sort of thing.'

'It depends,' he countered. 'It depends on how it's done.'

'So how have you done it, then?'

By stealth, thought Duncan. I've done it by stealth. But he answered, 'Sensible plotting, that's the key, Shirl. You wouldn't believe the stupid things people do in plays. That Othello, now, he kills his missus because she loses a hankie!'

'Crikey!' said Shirley, sliding back under the duvet. 'Hankies always go missing down the launderette.'

'Oh, they do such stupid things on stage.' Duncan turned away and prepared for sleep. 'But I've told them, mine's going to be a sensible play.'

Duncan sat at his desk needing words. It might be a week before Shirley began hinting, nagging, demanding again. To hasten her frustration into articulation, Duncan took his meals in the spare room.

'I'll have mine on a tray, Shirl. Can't stop. Act Two's at a crucial point.'

And as he waited to record her reaction, he read and re-read Act One. The Exposition: The meeting and marrying of the hero and heroine, alias Duncan and Shirley.

They met in the theatre where he worked part-time. An amateur production, but he hadn't let that dissuade him from helping Shirley serve the interval coffee nor agreeing to meet the following weekend. And the faces had approved.

'You need to experience love, Duncan, with all its exquisite emotion. Then you can write about it. Love will mould you into a playwright.'

Duncan wanted to tap the much-trumpeted source of inspiration and when Shirley guided his hand into soft folds and fissures he had only dreamt about, he became convinced he had.

'You're my inspiration, Shirl, my inspiration.'

But after their wedding, the honeymoon and setting up home in a dingy maisonette no plot or words came easily. Duncan was not unhappy, but married life did not inspire him. It was just too busy. There was a daily list of jobs lined up for him on the kitchen jotter, the big shop every Friday, and a rota of weekend visits to relatives and friends. Shirley proved unimpressed with his literary ambition, immune to his life plan, unmoved by his plea for writing time.

'But I thought *you* had aspirations, Shirl.'

'I've got aspirations all right, and they start with you getting a proper job.'

Proper job. Proper job. A recurring comment. A constant lament. But even worse, Shirley preferred television to live theatre.

'Telly's much more cosy, Duncan.' She patted the settee beside her. 'More of a laugh, too.'

'What are you saying, Shirley? I saw you as a fellow thespian. A leading lady waiting in the wings for your big chance.'

No! No! No! She had been serving coffee when they met as a favour to a friend not because the drama group was flush with females.

'Honestly, Duncan, I never pretended otherwise. You just got hold of the wrong end of the stick as usual. Too much imagination, that's your trouble,'

Here was conflict and the inspiration Duncan had been seeking. He would develop it. He ignored Shirley's invitation to watch the telly and her list of jobs. He began to write his script.

Act Two went slowly. The proper job chorus became repetitive. In a well-made play conflict should lead to crisis. A crisis Duncan must manufacture. He began sleeping in the spare room.

'I might need to work late, see Shirl. Don't want to disturb you. You have to be up early.'

'That might be easier,' said Shirley with a shrug of her shoulders, and locked their bedroom door.

Role reversal.

'Shirley! Open this door. I'm your husband.'

Hollow laughter.

'Open the door please, Shirl. I need you.'

Rising laughter.

'Shirl, you're my inspiration. Truly you are.'

Shirley opened the door.

'Inspiration!' she spat out the word. 'I'm flesh and blood, Duncan. I'm not for taking like a bottle of tonic. Go sleep with your sodding play.'

So Duncan slept with his play in the narrow camp bed under second-hand blankets. He lived with his play amid accumulating litter. Each day he sat at the mirror-less dressing table arranging and re-arranging sentences. He sought to resolve the plot, to bring about the denouement. He wanted a happy ending but the words would not come, because there were no words. No real words. Shirley refused to speak to him.

At the theatre the painted, powdered faces mocked him.

'What price your advice now, Duncan? You have to

unravel the plot before your play can feature in the hall of fame. You have to finish the script before your protagonist can become one of us.'

'I know that,' he said. 'I'm working on it. Working very hard if you must know.'

'Of course it's hard,' rejoined the faces. 'You think we had it easy? Why not listen to us, Duncan? Learn from our experience. Let us give you good advice.'

'No thanks. I've seen the stupid things you lot get up to. Complication upon complication. I'll skip your advice, thank you.'

Then, suddenly, Duncan was skipping, doing a little dancing jig of joy.

'Are you all right?' The faces were concerned. 'We've never seen you like this before.'

'Inspiration!' Duncan rejoiced. 'The spark from heaven. That's what's happened. No need for advice now. I've thought of the denouement. I've got the ending. I know what to do.'

Duncan danced down the stairs and out through the stage door. The crisis was resolved. The end writ large. A climax so simple Duncan wondered why he hadn't thought of it before. A resolution of his own making. Not stolen, copied or cloned. All his own work. He hurried home to tell Shirley.

But home was an anti-climax. An empty stage. No lighting. No co-star.

Duncan knocked on the door of their room.

'You in there, Shirl? Can I come in?'

No reply but the door was unlocked. An open door, thought Duncan, is an invitation. He would warm a place for Shirley as he had in the early days of their marriage. He undressed and climbed into their double bed. Clean sheets. Soft duvet. Shirley's nightdress neatly folded upon the pillow. And amid its folds – a handkerchief. A large white handkerchief embroidered with the initial 'L'.

Enter Shirley. High heels and lipstick.

'What are you doing here, Duncan?'

'What is this doing here?' He held out the handkerchief as if it were contaminated, one corner gripped between thumb and forefinger.

'The flag of surrender,' quipped Shirley. 'You want a truce?'

'The truth, strumpet, I want the truth. Who does this belong to? Who's this 'L' that's been having you?'

'Give over the dramatics, Duncan. I'm not in the mood. Anyway, what do you care?'

He cared. He cared she was spoiling the ending.

'Who is he?' Duncan shouted. He seized Shirley by the throat and shook her hard. 'I'll have it out of you. So help me, I will …'

'I… found… it… laund… er… ette …' gasped Shirley, choking for breath.

Passion. Power. Pressure. Pace. And then a pause. And in the pause Duncan's quavering voice.

'Shirley? Wake up, Shirl … Please, Shirl, wake up. I want you to hear the play. Our play. We'll read it together. Leading man and leading lady.'

Duncan read the play to Shirley, lifting and lightening his voice when he took her part. Act One. Interval coffee. Act Two.

'It's good. Don't you think so. Shirl?'

But Shirley did not applaud. She lay propped up on a pillow, a necklace of purple bruises about her neck.

'You recognise bits here and there,' continued Duncan. 'Of course you do. But Act Three's all my own work. No eavesdropping. Honest. I worked it out all by myself. This is what happens. You watch now, Shirl.'

And he tore up the script. Rent scenes apart. Severed sentences, phrases, single words. Slowly. Deliberately. Page after page. Beyond reconstruction.

'My decision, Shirl. A proper job. Nine to five. Time together.'

Faces. Faces ascending to the gods, descending to the pit. Duncan knew these faces. Knew them well enough to tell the truth. He told Othello he understood about the handkerchief. He confessed he could not finish his play.

'I realise now, it isn't easy to keep to a sensible plot.'

'Not easy at all,' said the faces. 'If you're a real character you're not going to let a playwright push you around. You like to spring a few surprises. Cause complications.'

'There were complications.'

'We tried to warn you. Playwrights don't get everything their own way. It's the unexpected that creates drama.'

'I discovered the unexpected in myself,' Duncan sobbed. 'I discovered passion … and love …'

'Then you must use this experience,' the faces insisted.

'No! Never! No more writing.'

'You mustn't give up, Duncan. We've told you, we're happy to give advice. Why not listen to …'

'You listen!' Duncan held up his hand for silence. Off stage the distant wail of a police siren. 'That's my cue. I'm leaving the theatre. I just came in to say goodbye.'

'Then take your bow. It's well deserved. You've turned in a sparkling performance and kept us all very presentable.'

The faces were applauding him. Kings and commoners alike. Duncan picked up his cleaning cloths, his mop and his bucket and tried to make a proper job of his exit.

THE CUCKOO CHILD

I believed Titania to be my mother. Why wouldn't I? She mirrored the care other woodland creatures gave their young. I wanted for nothing. At her command the sweetest milk was served, fresh berries picked and new-laid eggs plucked warm from the nest.

Of course I thought she was my mother. It was to her I turned when frightened by a darkening sky, the call of the screech-owl or a barking fox. She held me close and calmed my infant fears.

'Don't be afraid, little prince. Nothing shall harm you here.'

She sang lullabies as I curled into sleep and ordered me sweet dreams.

But as I grew in boyhood confidence and learning, doubt wriggled into those dreams like worm in pretty toadstools. Titania, queen of the woodland folk, treated me as her little prince, but the king, Oberon, ignored me. He seemed irritated by my presence. Was this any way for a father to behave? And how strange that my skin shone nut-brown when theirs was as pale as the dainty anemone.

'Foolish boy,' chided Puck, the king's jester. 'Look close at the world hereabout and you will see the answer to your riddle.'

Puck was a mischief-maker but he was good at riddles so I took his advice. When in the company and tutelage of Titania's attendants, I made great play of my interest in her kingdom. I pleaded to go on walks, to explore, to observe and question my expanding world. And I saw that infant creatures – whether born in tree, den, bush or burrow – grew to resemble their parents. All save one; the cuckoo bird became much bigger and stronger, and of quite a different song and feather. How could this be?

'That bird,' said Peas-Blossom, 'is a lazy cheat who does not raise or care for its young.'

'Then who does?' I was puzzled.

'Another bird,' answered Cobweb. 'The cheating cuckoo has many tricks under its wing.'

'Let me explain,' said Moth.

'No!' Mustard-Seed stood forward. 'I will tell the little …'

'Enough you hot-head!' Peas-Blossom held up a warning finger. 'No more now. We've wandered too far.'

'Tell me about the cuckoo,' I pleaded.

'Another day,' said Mustard-Seed as we turned to retrace our steps. 'The queen will be waiting.'

We came upon the royal quarrel on our return. Oberon stalked past us, unsmiling, tight-lipped, his face like thunder. Titania flounced away in the opposite direction declaring, 'I have forsworn his bed and company.'

Puck told us that Oberon was very angry. He and Titania had argued so long and so bitterly that now they would no longer hold court together.

'Angry indeed,' said Mustard-Seed, 'his face could curdle milk.'

'And will do so,' said Puck, 'and call up sea fogs and maladies.'

Peas-Blossom frowned. 'This strife will cause confusion everywhere and hardship is bound to follow.'

'But why?' I turned to my four tutors. 'Why should my parents quarrel so?'

No-one answered. They looked away. One by one they left to attend their queen.

'Foolish boy,' Puck whispered in my ear. 'Listen to those around you and you will hear the answer.'

The jester seemed intent on helping me so I took his advice. I edged close to any passing woodland folk as I played. I pretended to be absorbed in childish pursuits while listening to their gossip. All the tittle-tattle was of the rift between Titania and Oberon. I heard of things I did not fully understand – fogs and floods, sick animals and failing crops in a world outside the wood. Some blamed Oberon, others Titania.

'The king is passing fell and wrath.'

'He has good reason for the queen defies his majesty.'

'She could put a stop to all this confusion but refuses to obey.'

'Because she loves her little Indian boy and will not give him up.'

'She ignores tradition and everyone suffers for her folly.'

Some took the king's side, others held with the queen, but all blamed the little Indian boy.

'The queen makes him all her joy.'

'He's a cuckoo child who hasn't flown the nest.'

'Aye, a boy his age needs a master.'

And they looked toward where I was playing. Were they talking about me?

I sought out Master Mustard-Seed.

'Tell me now about the cuckoo bird. Does it really get another to raise its young?'

'It does.'

'But how?'

'When the green leaves are showing, the cuckoo comes looking.' Mustard-Seed mimed a bird flying hither and thither. 'When it spies an unattended nest of eggs down it swoops. It sucks those eggs dry and lays one of its own in their place. Then off it flies to enjoy a life of leisure.'

I applauded his play-acting.

'And the other birds don't realise?'

'No. The hapless pair raise the intruder as their own while, nearby, the canny cuckoo mocks them with its cry. Cuckoo! Cuckoo!'

'Thank you, Mustard-Seed. I understand now why the cuckoo has different feathers from its parents.' I gave a little bow. 'And is that why the king and queen are fair and I am dark? Am I a cuckoo child?'

The colour drained from Mustard-Seed's florid face.

'Little prince, you are as crafty as the cuckoo.' Unsmiling, he returned my bow. 'I will say no more, so be done with your tricks.'

'I'm sorry, Mustard-Seed.' I pulled at his sleeve to prevent him from leaving. 'But I hear the prattle of the court about a little Indian boy who is the cause of all this strife, and I'm sure they're talking about me.'

'Your ears are befuddling you.' Mustard-Seed said kindly. 'The queen loves you. That is all you need to know.'

'But the king does not.' I countered. 'Why? What have I done wrong?'

'Nothing, little prince.'

'You call me prince but do I deserve such a title?'

'You are a prince.' Mustard-Seed smiled. 'I can tell you that and so will the queen if you ask her.'

But I could not ask her. The words froze on my tongue and the ice found its way to my heart. I was no longer a mewling infant seeking Titania's comfort, but a wayward boy wanting to prove his growing prowess and test a mother's love. I saw Mustard-Seed frown at my ingratitude and disobedience and, finally, his temper got the better of his tongue.

'If you are not careful, young sir, you will find yourself in Oberon's train.'

'What d'you mean?' I demanded.

'I mean that Oberon wants you for his page.'

I was shocked into silence. The king wanted me to attend on him as a page! My childish goading had given me an answer, but not the one I wanted. Oberon could not be my father. I had no father that I knew.

'Tell me, Mustard-Seed,' I blinked away my tears, 'what father makes his son a servant? I know now that I am not a prince.'

Good Master Mustard-Seed said nothing but took my hand, dried my tears and walked me to the queen.

Titania sat in her woodland bower weaving purple columbine into her long, fair hair. She greeted us with a smile and out-stretched arms. 'Welcome, my little prince.' But I could not run to embrace her for Mustard-Seed held me by the shoulders.

'Forgive my impertinence, milady queen,' he said, 'but I must speak to you on a matter that heats up my head and so burns my heart I can no longer keep silent.'

'What is it, Mustard-Seed?'

'Your boy here is undone by woodland gossip. He thinks himself a cuckoo child and not a prince.'

'How so? Has that knavish jester of the king been put to making mischief?'

'Milady, the mischief is in keeping the boy a babe. He

is grown in years and old enough for knowledge of himself. If you do not speak, he will fashion answers of his own from the unkind tittle-tattle of the court.'

Titania did not answer. Mustard-Seed gripped my shoulders tighter. Then Titania beckoned.

'Come and sit with me, my little prince. We must talk.'

Mustard-Seed let me go.

I am a prince. Not an Indian boy, but an Indian prince. Titania has told me this. She has given me the truth of who I am. She has told me that I am a child of the mortal world; the world beyond her kingdom. I was born beside a great ocean in a distant land; born to a mother who died giving me life, for such calamity can happen in the human sphere. I survived because my mother had been a friend and devoted follower of Titania and she took care of me.

'You are safe with me, little prince,' she said. 'I will not give you up for all of fairyland.'

I lamented the loss of two mothers and then wondered if the cuckoo chick felt as I did. Fed and cared for but a misfit in its cosy nest. It finds the courage to fly when fully grown. Will I be able to do the same? Will I ever leave this woodland kingdom and return to my own world; to my own people?

I asked Puck about the land of India for he boasts often of his travels and conjures cloud shapes of the sights he's seen to entertain his listeners.

'Last time I flew there,' he said, 'I spied your father riding atop an elephant – both were bejewelled and glistening in the sun.'

'My father?' I gasped.

'And walking in attendance many servants playing golden horns and cymbals as befits a king in that noisy, hot and spicy land.' He paused and then added, 'A king who still mourns his wife and child.'

'He thinks me dead?'

'Of course. Titania stole you from your mother's side and fashioned a changeling in your place that seemed to live but for a moment.'

'I thought she was my mother's friend.' I am too bitter for tears.

'She was,' said Puck with sudden kindness, 'and she loves you because of that but, if she loves our realm, she must give you up.'

'To serve Oberon.'

'It is expected. The king has plans for you.'

'Titania will not give me up.'

Puck smiled that sly, mischievous smile of his. 'Neither the queen nor your four guardians are any match for Oberon.' And then he was gone.

And so it proved. I know not how this was brought about only that Oberon's magic was the stronger. There were mortals in the wood one summer night and I thought to escape with them. But my plan was undone by an ass of a man with whom Titania fell blindly in love. No doubt Puck had a hand in bringing this about. He thinks mortal men are fools but he made his queen a fool. So smitten was she with this monster that when Oberon asked for me again, Titania readily agreed. She gave me up to be alone in the embrace of her new love, to sing him songs and weave garlands around his ungainly ears. She gave me up without a murmur and I was sent under escort to my new master.

I now serve in Oberon's train – his nut-brown Indian page. He and Titania are reconciled so she makes no protest. There is no longer discord in the woodland court or in the other solid world. I am no longer the subject of gossip but, in this pale company, I am plainly a cuckoo child. I dream of a noisy, hot and spicy land. I dream that one day I shall ride upon an elephant.

WAITING FOR MICHAEL

The Reverend Minister's house stands close to the east wall of the churchyard. If I take position atop an old stone vault I can watch him walking in his garden. I can eavesdrop on his conversation. That is how I hear about the wedding.

'I do congratulate you both,' enthuses the vicar.

He is talking to a young couple, both fair and handsome, both strangers to me.

'Yours will be the first wedding in the church for … well, for a very long time.'

'How extraordinary,' exclaims the young woman. 'It's such a lovely setting.'

'Exactly how long?' asks the young man.

The vicar hesitates, as well he might. 'I would need to check the records to be absolutely certain,' he replies, 'but some considerable time.'

I've been waiting for Michael all that considerable time. I wait at the lych-gate, willing Michael to come full stride up Stoke Greenford's cobbled street. But it's the village women who come gossiping towards the church and I flee from their cruel tongues. I retreat into the churchyard and wait at the gate that looks northward to the fens. If Michael has been delayed he will come this way. He will take the short cut across the old causeway – a path known only to fenmen and smugglers in need of sanctuary.

'I'll wait,' I tell my father when he comes in search of me.

'It's no good, girl,' he replies. 'Come home.'

'I'll wait,' I say again. 'I'll wait a little longer.'

But then I hear my mother and her entourage coming from the church. She's fretting about the boiled bacon and the vegetables that will go to waste. I had chided Michael for laughing at her preoccupation with food, but now my Mother's kitchen concern makes me weep. I do not stop to greet her. Out of the North gate I run, along the causeway and across the fens to Michael's cottage. The door is locked. The windows barred.

My father and brother find me there. They find me tearing at my petticoats like a half-demented midwife. But it's not to staunch blood, not to stem a haemorrhage that I tear strips of calico. I clean the cottage windows. I mop the salt mist from the glass as if the pure whiteness of the cloth can change the emptiness I see within. I wipe and rub and polish, hoping the blue embroidered forget-me-nots can conjure Michael working at his easel.

'Come home, girl,' says my father. 'There's nothing for you here.'

And he and my brother prise me gently from my toil and take me back along the causeway.

A sorry sight I look now in my made-to-measure grey silk. The hand-stitched skirt is ringed with dirt and fenland damp. The delicate shell-shaped buttons are lost or broken and a ragged hem of calico trails in my wake.

'Hold yer head up, girl,' chides my father. 'You've nothing to be ashamed of.'

But I sense the solitary bittern hiding in the reeds, watching our sad procession. It stretches its neck skyward but keeps an accusing eye on me.

'I see you,' it booms forth. 'And I saw what you did with Michael.'

At home my mother has taken charge. She is slicing bacon and urging vegetables upon friends and relations gathered around her table.

'Best take off that dress,' she commands, 'and then come and sit down. I don't want good food going to waste.'

'No,' I answer, defiantly. 'I'll keep the dress till Michael comes.'

'You're in no fit state to sit at table,' argues Mother, but Father intervenes.

'This were meant to be a wedding feast,' he says, leading me to my bridal chair. 'The girl can wear her wedding dress if she's a mind to.'

The vicar leads his visitors to their chairs as his wife sets tea upon the garden table.

'So you're the brave young couple,' she declares. 'Defying village tradition. Challenging the Grey Lady.'

'Nothing of the kind,' retorts the vicar. 'They're just getting married.'

He is annoyed at his wife's interference and so am I. I want to play at Jack O' Lantern, to be Will O' the Wisp again. It's some years since I danced a bridegroom through the bogs and misty marshes.

'Who is the Grey Lady?' enquire the young couple.

I am the Grey Lady. I am waiting for Michael in my pearl-grey gown. He will come for me and I must stand ready to celebrate our marriage.

'See what your softness has done,' my mother nags my father. 'Lord knows when she'll take that dress off now.'

'She'll come to herself in time,' replies father. 'Just leave her be.'

But mother shakes her head.

'She were too certain, too smitten,' she mutters as she busies herself in the kitchen. 'The shock has curdled her brain.'

Stoke Greenford is abuzz with whispers. I hear them all around me like a swarm of flies on carrion. Whispers that Michael had never intended marriage. Whispers that his journey to the coast to sell his paintings had been a well devised plan of escape. Whispers that I had bewitched him with the scent of yarrow flower and that once free of my company, the memory of his true love had returned.

The bosoms of the village women heave as they suck in and hold back their gossip while I pass by. They do not look me in the face but their eyes and their opinions follow me down the narrow streets. I should have taken good advice, not put my trust in strangers nor thought myself a cut above wedding a local lad. The children are different. They don't whisper as they parade me to church. They chant, 'Mad Martha. Mad Martha.' at the top of their voices and try to stamp upon my trail of calico.

'According to tradition,' the vicar's wife persists as she pours the tea, 'the poor girl was jilted on her wedding day and ever since …'

'Ever since,' interrupts her husband, 'people have let their imagination run riot.'

I need only step from the covering wings of the vault's stone angel to disabuse him of that fallacy. I am tempted but decide to bide hidden. I'm eager for this wedding to be arranged. I fancy the fair young man has the look of an artist. He reminds me much of Michael. I could let my imagination run riot whilst leading this bridegroom a merry dance.

'Now, my dear,' the vicar's wife scolds gently. 'You may

scoff at such things, naturally enough, but I do think these young people have a right to know. It is their wedding, after all.'

'What do we have a right to know?' the couple ask simultaneously.

The vicar sighs.

'I suppose if I don't tell you, someone in the village will.'

Someone in the village tells tales to my mother. 'Are you with child?' she demands. 'Is that what all this madness is about?'

I lie. I lie to my mother for the first time in my nineteen years and the false words come easily.

'I am not with child.'

'Then let the past go,' she pleads. 'Change out that dress and stop moping about the churchyard.'

'Michael's been delayed, that's all,' I insist. 'He'll be back soon. I know he will. You'll see.'

But the delay lengthens and Michael sends no message, no word of explanation. The fury inside me grows with the child – secret and unseen at first but breaking forth as I feel the grey silk tighten around my waist. I rage at the whispering village, lash out at its chanting children. I upbraid my family for unsettling Michael with their fenland talk and their country manners. My brother brings tidings I will not accept.

He returns from the coast with news that Michael had indeed sold his paintings, but that not a soul had seen him thereafter or knew his present whereabouts. I blaspheme when the Reverend Minister attempts to end my churchyard vigil. I struggle. I shout. I call upon the ancient fenland gods. I swear aloud that no-one will marry in his church till I have news of Michael. I hear the young man gasp in surprise.

'You mean there hasn't been a wedding here since the last century?'

The vicar puts down his piece of fruit cake. 'Oh, please don't let this change your minds.' He smiles encouragingly. 'It only needs one couple – one bright, modern, educated couple like yourselves – to nail this silly superstition.'

I, too, hope the betrothed won't turn chapel or go to the neighbouring parish. Then this silly minister will see the power of his so-called superstition.

'But surely,' argues the young woman, 'There's something more.'

She's right. The Reverend Minister – as is the wont of reverend ministers – has told them only half a tale.

'I read history at university,' she continues, 'and folk lore was my special study. I doubt poor Martha's lovesick raving could start such a long-standing superstition. There's something you haven't told us.'

I haven't told my mother I'm with child. She accepts my word and encourages my new-found appetite.

'Eat well and you'll get well,' she says, setting a full plate before me.

I pretend to need the comfort of her food and eat heartily to explain my thickening waistline. But before I take to my lonely bed I find a quiet, hidden place and vomit away the excess. The deceit does not worry me. Michael will be here before I'm seen to be a liar. He will take me away from this place of ridicule and gossip. I keep watch for him each day during the hours permitted for marriage. I tell the Reverend Minister I have as much right in the churchyard as any other villager. I tell my father the same. If people are troubled by my appearance they can avert their eyes. I intend waiting for Michael.

Stoke Greenford goes about its business while I sit on an old stone vault and demand of an impotent angel why my prayers go unanswered.

A voice behind me says, 'Martha, it grieves me to see you like this.'

I don't bother to turn round. It's not Michael's voice. It's Thomas, my erstwhile sweetheart.

'Are you looking for someone?' I challenge. 'Give me their name. I'll pinpoint where they rest in peace.'

'I've come to see you, Martha.'

I smile at Thomas' dog-like devotion. 'Fancy your chances now, I warrant.'

'No, Martha. I've come to ask a favour.'

'My favours are all spoken for,' I say tartly. 'What is it you want, Thomas?'

'I'm to wed this Saturday,' he replies. 'I want for you to stop at home.'

The fury inside me freezes cold. I turn to Thomas with a look more potent than a full field of magic yarrow flower.

They take Thomas up out the marsh and carry his sodden body home.

'I didn't do it,' I shout at the whisperers. 'It was for shame. He were sore ashamed.'

But they don't believe me. They draw back as I pass and clasp their children close. They are afraid. They are afraid of Mad Martha. I see their fear. I feel it. I delight in it. The power to hurt has passed to me.

'I told you,' I boast gleefully. 'I told you. No wedding, no bridal vows till I have news of Michael.'

The legacy of witch-pricking lingers long in this locality. I'm blamed for everything that goes wrong in the village from spoilt butter to insect bites. My clout increases with every calamity.

'You must put her away,' the Reverend Minister instructs my parents.

'I won't go,' I bawl at him, 'and neither you nor your God can make me.'

'She must be put away,' he repeats, ignoring my outburst. 'For her own safety she must be put away. She must ...' his voice drops to a whisper, 'be certified.'

'A little more time,' argues father. 'She'll come to herself given time.'

'I'm building her up,' adds my mother. 'Good, wholesome food. Never fails. She's filling out nicely.'

The minister's accusing finger trembles as he points out my shame.

'She's with child, woman,' he cries. 'She's full with child not food. And there's them in the village say she's bedded Beelzebub.'

The young couple are attentive to my story. I like that the young woman is anxious for me.

'What happened to her?' she asks.

'She was found floating in the marsh like Thomas,' replies the Vicar. 'Her death is recorded as suicide.'

'But you're not convinced.'

The vicar shrugs.

'Who can tell? Let's just say that country folk have ways and means of meting out their own punishment.'

'So now she haunts the churchyard seeing off prospective bridegrooms,' laughs the young man.

'Irrational nonsense.' The Vicar joins in the merriment.

'Classic development of a superstition,' says the young woman and smiles at her beloved. 'You'll survive.'

'I just thought you should know,' says the Vicar's wife, defensively. 'Even the most rational tend to get a bit superstitious on their wedding day. Think of "Something old, something new . . ."'

' "Something borrowed, something blue",' concludes the young woman. 'Symbols that have become tradition.'

'Just tradition,' agrees her intended.

'See,' the vicar smiles triumphantly. 'These two aren't superstitious. They're children of their time.'

I smile. I've heard persuasive ministers before. They never tell the full story. They acknowledge Thomas, but ignore the others. They think the ancient magic was drained away with the fen water. I hear enough to lay my plans. I turn to descend from the vault when the young woman exclaims, 'I'd like to find out what happened to Michael.'

I stay my descent and turn back.

'Why should we assume he jilted Martha?' she demands. 'If it was common knowledge he'd sold his paintings that could well have led to problems.'

She speaks my words. Echoes my arguments.

'Those were dangerous times. He might have been robbed, beaten senseless for the money in his purse.'

She gives my answers to the whisperers who would not listen.

'Perhaps he lay ill – taken in somewhere or picked up by travellers. Perhaps he sent word when it was too late.' She takes the young man's arm and pulls him close. 'Let's do some research, darling. This Michael was a fellow artist. There should be some paintings and possibly other records.'

Oh, give me news, young woman. Give me news and I'll give you your bridegroom. I remain to watch the lovers take their leave.

'You'll find Martha's gravestone alongside the north wall,' the Vicar tells them. 'On the fen side, of course. She rests in unconsecrated ground.'

The Reverend Minister is wrong again.

I do not rest.

I am waiting for Michael.

THE POPPY FIELD

Mothers rarely know their children as well as they think they do. Mine thinks she knows what's best for me, but I disagree. I'm old enough to look after myself and intend to lead my own life whatever she says.

I had to accept her mother-hen act when I was younger but, even as a child, I found it irksome. I wanted to stay out late, to visit the landscape of the night and dance under its dark skies, but Mother always called me home well before sunset.

'Persephone! Persephone!'

The panic rose in her voice in a tone which told me I had power and could make bargains.

'Per...seph...on...e!'

I would disobey until there came a sob in her voice and then I'd run to her, pretending to have only just heard and offering wild flowers. Mother would scoop me into her arms, carry me indoors and to my bed. There she warned me against wandering all alone at night and particularly in the field where the poppies grew.

Mother didn't know me very well then, nor does she

now. I've never been afraid of the dark and I love the rich red poppies with their crinkled petals as thin as butterfly wings.

They flutter in the corn like a trickle of blood on sun-kissed skin.

'No!' Mother screams. 'Ye gods, no.' She snatches away the knife. 'What are you doing? Are you mad?'

She need not have worried. I intended only one cut. One small cut to make my argument. She binds the wound on my arm, comforting and berating me in turn.

'It's just a scratch,' I say. 'Nothing to get alarmed about.'

'But why? Why?'

'You bind me with invisible bonds. I need to cut myself free.'

And so I win. I come and go as I please while Mother fusses over her plants and flowers. Her warnings are silent now but loud enough in the clutch of her hands and troubled eyes. Every evening she watches from the garden gate as I go in search of the bustling nightlife in our neighbouring town. Before the path turns away into the poppy field, I wave a cheerful but eager farewell. Her hand flutters and falls. She is afraid of the dark, afraid for me, but I'm not worried. I welcome the night in all its silhouette and shadow. It hides much imperfection. It comforts me.

I stay out later and later to prove there's nothing to fear. I know the sounds which follow me home – the scurrying and the rustling – are but wild creatures who, like me, prefer the dark. And, on the poppy field path, I stop to listen to the muted revels of Mother's worst fear – the music of a notorious nightclub carried faintly on the midnight air. I long to join the revellers in that hidden place, to dance to the beat of their music and share their secrets, but I know no-one to invite me.

'Its the in place to be,' I tell Mother, 'but membership is so exclusive. I need an invitation.'

'Skulking about in the dark,' she rants, 'ashamed to show themselves in the light of day. Why would you want such people as friends?'

But I want the forbidden. I want admission to the Poppy Field Club.

I decide to dress in black. It demands attention like the bold, black heart of the poppy.

'But why?' asks Mother. 'You are young. It's old women who wear black.'

She takes me to her garden, shows me the summer flowers.

'These are new to the world. Look at their colours.' She lovingly cups each chosen bloom to show bright against her palm. Pink. Yellow. Orange. Blue. 'And see the different shades of green.' She gathers leaves to show me.

'Young life wears such colours,' says Mother. 'Black is for the old who mourn their youth.'

'I've heard black is worn at the Poppy Field.'

She lets the leaves drop.

'You keep away from that place.'

'I go where I want,' I shout, 'and I wear what I want. It's my life.' And I'm away through the gate and do not look back.

I put on my new dress and smooth its silk over my body. The low cut neckline reveals a hint of cleavage, and clever darts and tucks accentuate my waist and hips. Black suits me. I tie a red sash around my waist and apply matching colour to my lips.

'Oh, Persephone, you look so grown up, no longer my little girl.'

'Exactly! I am grown up.' I spit out the words. 'I'm no longer anybody's little girl. And I want to be called Sephy from now on.'

I leave Mother in her garden. She leans over the gate calling,

'Take care. Take care. Take care.'

I rarely meet anyone on my way to town but this evening I see a man on the far side of the poppy field. If he's going to the club this might be my chance; he might take me with him. Mother's warning echoes in my mind, but my black dress confidence over-rides it. I wave. He salutes in return, calls that I should wait and hurries to join me.

'Who is this lovely young lady?'

He's handsome, swarthy, and dressed in black. He looks at me as Mother looks at her flowers. I enjoy the admiration.

'I'm Sephy.'

'Little black dress, eh?' he says. 'Very nice, Sephy. Very nice. Going somewhere special?'

'Maybe,' I tease.

'The Poppy Field, perhaps?'

'Maybe.'

He comes closer. I feel his breath on my cheek.

'More like wanna-be. I've heard on the town grapevine that you walk this path every evening hoping for a chance of admittance.'

'Yes,' I acknowledge.

I feel his warmth. I'm drawn to his manliness.

'I've seen you here. You linger in the shadow and listen to the music.' He takes me in his arms. 'And you long to dance.'

'Yes.'

He dances me back and forth along the path. I've never been so close to a man. I respond to his touch and to his kiss.

'Sephy – a little night bird looking for the Poppy Field.'

'Yes.'

'Lingering. Longing.'

My head rests against his chest.

'Yes. Yes.'

'And tonight your wishes come true.'

He twirls me from the path and into the poppies. Their black hearts nod encouragingly as he lays me down. I feel the hardness of his body and cry at the brutal beauty of it and the certain knowledge that I can call myself a grown woman.

He helps me to my feet and I scrabble up my discarded clothes. My hands shake as I retie my red sash, straighten my dress and brush off the dirt.

'Now I'll take you to the club,' he says. 'You've earned your entrance fee.'

'I should go home.' I continue fussing over my dress. 'My mother waits up.'

He laughs.

'Waiting and worrying are a mother's two apron strings. Grown girls should recognise emotional blackmail and learn to deal with it.'

I know it to be true. I've longed to break those ties and to join the Poppy Field revels.

'Can you really get me membership?'

'Maybe.' His arm goes round my waist, tight and controlling. 'I'm teasing. Of course I can. I say who's in and who's out at the Poppy Field, and I want you there.'

'And I want to be there.'

He scoops me up and hurries me away from my homeward path all the while singing the praises of the night and the plant of joy.

He is strong and makes light work of carrying me. I snuggle my face against his shoulder and take no note of guiding landmarks. I hear him quieten a guard dog and then he sets me down. We are standing at the top of a steep flight of stone steps, each tread illuminated with ice-blue light. Now the familiar music of the midnight air is close and distinct. I tremble at its nearness.

'Don't be afraid. You're safe with me.'

He takes my hand and we descend. A door opens and closes behind us.

This is a new world to me. The infamous club, hidden away in underground caverns beneath the poppies. It's dimly lit, plushly furnished and loud with the throb of music and the noisy excitement of carefree people.

'Welcome to the club.' He guides me to a table. 'My own little kingdom.'

'It's wonderful … so vibrant … so alive. Can I dance?'

'Until you drop, but go clean up first.' He snaps his fingers and is surrounded by squabbling women pawing at him with no sense of shame.

Dance with me, Pluto.

'It's my turn.'

'Says who, you bitch?'

'Back off, girls,' he orders. 'I'm with Sephy now. One of you show her to the powder room.'

They slink away and the slowest is obliged to carry out his command.

I return to the table – my hair combed, lipstick reapplied and confidence restored.

'Dance with me, Pluto.'

'The house cocktail first.' He hands me a wine glass. 'It'll give you staying power.'

I drink it down, impatient to be on the dance floor. It's like nothing I've tasted before. A sensation of warmth rushes through me. I am alive and free. This is where I'm meant to be and I love it. I dance and dance and dance until I drop exhausted into Pluto's arms.

I lie naked in a huge bed dressed with black silk sheets. Am I awake or am I dreaming? My eyes are wide open; my body lies heavy; my head throbs. Suddenly, hundreds of white and worm-like roots come wriggling through the roof of the cavern from the poppy field above. They creep down the walls and seek me out, curling about my limbs, holding me down, taking sustenance from my body. I cry out and tear at my arms and legs as I struggle to be free. Then Pluto is there.

'Hush now, Sephy, it's just a bad trip. This will help.'

I am Pluto's woman now. I share his bed and his nightclub life. Other members must defer to me and some are green with envy.

'Don't worry, you're the queen bee here,' he says. 'A Pluto must have a Persephone.'

He shares with me the secret of the poppy's tears. I crave that secret even more than I desire his body. My former life recedes, becomes faint in my memory. I recall very little – just occasionally a woman's voice calling, 'Take care. Take care. Take care.'

And then that voice wailing in my ear.

'Oh, what have they done to you? Wake up, Persephone … wake up … wake up.'

I'm slapped and shaken into consciousness and the woman pulls me from Pluto's bed. Her strong arms support me.

'She could have died, you wicked man. I'm taking her home this minute and don't you dare stop me.'

I look to Pluto for help but he offers none. His lips brush against my forehead and he whispers, 'Go with your mother now. You'll be back before too long and I'll be waiting for you.'

I half-remember this place, this locked room, this woman who tends my sickness. She holds me close when I cannot sleep for the trembling in my limbs. She wipes dribble from my nose and mouth when I cannot stop from crying. She bathes my dirty body, restrains my restlessness and soothes my mind with lullabies. Slowly the craving that gnawed at my very being subsides and leaves me.

'Mother?' I venture.

'Oh, my darling child, you're back.' She holds me close. 'I've been so lost without you.'

The door is unlocked and the world is open to me once more. Mother lays freshly laundered clothes on my bed. I choose a pale green shift to please her.

'I've not worn this for ages.'

She smiles.

'You always looked so lovely in it.'

I note the past tense. I'm not so lovely now and the dress hangs on me like a sack.

'You just need building up,' Mother adds hastily. 'Lots of good food, fresh air and early nights will soon have you looking beautiful again.'

I hesitate before facing the day. I've been a night person for so long.

'Don't be afraid,' says Mother. 'I'm right here.'

She opens the door and I step into the garden.

'What has happened?' I cry.

There is no garden. No flowers. No order. Only a wasteland of weeds.

'I thought you loved your garden?'

'I loved you more. It meant nothing after you'd gone.'

'Oh, Mother, then why couldn't you let me grow like your flowers? You didn't try to order their shape or colour.'

'Can't you understand I wasn't trying to shape you? I was trying to keep you safe.' She is close to tears. 'Even as a little girl you were reckless. You never saw danger, never heeded warnings. Such a wilful child! I never had a minute's peace until you were in your bed.' She takes a deep breath to stop from weeping. 'When you didn't come home that night, I knew what had happened. I just left everything and went into town. I walked the streets for weeks on end looking for you; asking, begging, offering bribes to anyone who would get me into that hellish place.'

I can't help a wry smile.

'Pluto's very good at security … among other things.'

There's a flash of Mother's old anger.

'And if it hadn't been for the girl, you might be very dead, like this garden.'

'What girl?'

I picture one of the pawing, green-eyed entourage in Pluto's bed. My place usurped.

'I don't know her name. She took my money, swore me to secrecy and smuggled me in. Just in time, thank heavens!'

Just in time. I must remember that, let it be my mantra. I must keep it in mind, that and the loss of time – time enough for a garden to wither and me with no sense of its passing.

'I can get back to a bit of gardening now you're on the mend,' says Mother. 'And it would do you good to help.'

I get the sun on my skin and dirt under my nails as I work with Mother to clear weeds and replant the garden, but always she calls a halt to our work before sundown.

'Supper time, Persephone.' She takes my arm and walks me indoors.

She is afraid again and her fear will soon outweigh her love. It is a fear that will stifle me. It is a fear that is growing strong and showy – as are her garden flowers. Pink. Yellow. Orange. Blue. I note there are no poppies of any colour.

'No!' says Mother. 'No poppies!'

But I love the poppy with its black heart the colour of Pluto's bed-sheets. In nearby fields the standing corn is changing from sea-green to harvest gold and poppies flutter there like a trickle of blood on sun-kissed skin.

A CASE OF ALLITERATION

'It was a wet, windy Wednesday in the West Country. The champagne had been put on ice when …'

Champagne! A typical postprandial beverage for the masses, thought Detective Sergeant Wellow, wryly. But it would be champagne in Dilys Day's world. She was a champagne sort of writer. A Dilys Day story bubbled over with rich, elegant characters living in houses large enough to host a jet-set of subjects and to overawe parochial, plodding police officers.

'What do you make of that, Parker?'

'It was a wet, windy Wednesday …' began Detective Constable Parker.

'I can read, damn it, Parker,' interrupted the sergeant. 'What do you make of it?'

'Alliterative start to a new book, sir?

'Oh, very observant, Parker. Wet. Windy. Wednesday.'

'Yes, sir. Nice clean piece of A4 in the old typewriter and another best seller is underway.'

'Start of a work of literary realism as today is

Wednesday and it's wet.' Sergeant Wellow's tone was sarcastic. 'Care to hazard a guess as to how many inhabitants of this "scepter'd isle" drink champers after their lunch?'

'Well, sir,' countered Parker, 'Dilys Day obviously did.' He indicated a half-empty bottle of champagne in an ice-bucket on the study desk.

'A life-style gained by selling the notion that amateurs outsmart we professionals in crime detection. Living in cloud cuckoo land, laddie.'

'Lived, sir,' corrected Constable Parker. 'Past Tense.'

'Exactly so, Parker,' agreed Sergeant Wellow. 'Miss Day won't be creating any more coppers who can't sift evidence and go chasing after red herrings.'

Their attention returned to the body of Dilys Day seated at an antique desk and slumped forward onto an ancient typewriter. Her face, twisted sideways, jammed its keys. Her arms, bedangled with bracelets, hung lifeless.

'I hope you can sift evidence, Parker.'

'I hope so too, sir.'

'Pen to paper, Parker.'

'And precise preliminaries, sir.'

Parker began making notes. He'd learnt the value of Sergeant Wellow's insistence on meticulous detail: dates, times and even weather conditions. And he'd learnt more than detection from his superior. He'd learnt to recognise alliteration, the correct use of English grammar and a smattering of Shakespeare. Working with Detective Sergeant Wellow was an education.

'Looks like there was some sort of celebration,' suggested Parker as Sergeant Wellow scrutinised the ice-bucket.

'Hmmm. Care to hazard a guess as to the number of celebrants?'

Parker blushed. Three empty glasses stood on the study desk.

'Hardly a party as you understand the word, Parker,' said Sergeant Wellow and bent to sniff each glass.

'No, sir. D'you think the stuff was in the champagne, sir?'

'The stuff, Parker?' Sergeant Wellow's tone matched his raised eyebrows.

'Well, it looks like poison, sir. I had a dog took poison once and …'

'Make a note of your observations,' interrupted Sergeant Wellow, 'and then leave it to the lab boys.'

'Yes, sir.'

'And let's get on before they crowd us out.'

They moved around the spacious study completing their preliminary investigation. In the early days of their partnership Parker had queried the need for two sets of these scene of crime notes. The reply was succinct.

'I like putting pen to paper, Parker. Practice makes perfect. Detection demands detail.'

And detail included the contents of Dilys Day's drinks cabinet and her bookcase.

'She wrote a lot of books, sir,' said Parker, admiring the Dilys Day Collection.

'Prolific, Parker. Prolific is the word for someone who writes a lot.'

'And she died working. And all those words that would have become a book are as dead as she is.'

'Very good turn of phrase, Parker. Couldn't have put it better myself.'

'And no-one will ever know what happened when the champagne was put on ice.'

'Any one of these will tell you.' Sergeant Wellow ran his hand along the spines of the Dilys Day Collection. 'Formula writing. The butler did it.'

Dilys Day's housekeeper wiped a tear stained cheek with her ample apron. 'She was a lovely person,' she sighed. 'A lovely person.'

'Prolific,' agreed Constable Parker.

'I've read every one of her books,' continued the housekeeper. 'Every single one and some more than once.'

Sergeant Wellow winced. He studied the three members of Dilys Day's household assembled in the kitchen. Only Mrs. Giles, the housekeeper, looked at home there as she bustled about serving coffee. Jenkins, the butler, was younger than Sergeant Wellow had expected; he'd have no problem in finding a new position. It might not be so easy for Miss Fanshawe, the frail, ageing secretary. A fact she seemed to recognise. She warmed her thin hands against the coffee cup intoning,

'Oh, whatever will happen to us now?'

'I'm sorry we have to question you at a time like this,' said Sergeant Wellow, 'but it is necessary.'

'Oh, I know it is, sergeant.' Mrs. Giles took off her apron and seated herself at the kitchen table with the others. 'I told you, I've read all Miss Dilys's books.'

'I understand you found the body, Mr. Jenkins,' continued Sergeant Wellow.

'That's correct. I did.' Jenkin's voice was a smooth and cultured as his appearance.

'He came running down here into my kitchen,' added Mrs. Giles, 'a shouting and hollering and I ran straight up to the study, but as soon as I saw her I knew she was dead. "Don't touch anything," I said to Jenkins. "Don't touch a thing." I knew that was right from Miss Dilys's books.'

'Exactly right, Mrs. Giles,' agreed Constable Parker.

'And what time was this?' asked Sergeant Wellow.

'At five o'clock,' replied Jenkins. 'I always went to the study at five to ascertain if Madam required any refreshment.'

'Didn't she have the champagne?'

'Oh, Miss Dilys didn't drink much of that,' said Mrs. Giles. 'Didn't care for the bubbles. Just a glass or two for the launch.'

'The launch?' queried Sergeant Wellow.

'We always had champagne when Miss Day started a new book,' said Miss Fanshawe, staring into her coffee cup. 'I don't know what will happen now.'

'That's what I said,' declared Constable Parker.

Sergeant Wellow finished his coffee. 'There were only three glasses,' he said pointedly.

Jenkins answered the implied question. 'I didn't partake on this occasion. It was my afternoon off. I'd arranged to have lunch with friends.'

'You've an alibi, then,' chipped in Mrs. Giles. 'You're in the clear.'

'Did you see Miss Day before you left for this luncheon engagement?' continued the sergeant.

'No. Madam wasn't an early riser.'

'But she did have a word with you.' Mrs. Giles patted the butler's hand. 'That's a comfort.

'Madam spoke to me on the house phone,' explained Jenkins. 'She reminded me about the champagne. I put it on ice just before I left.'

'And you were back before five?'

Jenkin's smiled. 'At about a quarter to, sergeant. I left my friend's house at four-thirty. The drive here takes approximately fifteen minutes.'

Mrs. Giles busily re-filled the coffee cups.

'So Miss Fanshawe and I were the last to see her alive,' she exclaimed. 'You'll want to know about that, sergeant.

It was at the launch. We drank a toast to the coming book. It must have been about one when we left the study. That's right isn't it, Miss Fanshawe? Came down here for a bite of lunch and here we stopped.'

Miss Fanshawe nodded miserably.

'Neither of you returned to the study?

'Oh, no. The afternoons was Miss Dilys's creative time. No-one disturbed her afternoons. Quiet is very important for a writer.'

'Very true. Very true, Mrs. Giles,' said Sergeant Wellow getting up from the table. 'Thank you for the coffee. There's just one more thing. What was Miss Day's tipple seeing as she wasn't too keen on champagne?'

Constable Parker drove Sergeant Wellow back to their station.

'What was that drink again, sir?'

'Amaretto on the rocks.'

'That's a new one on me.'

Sergeant Wellow consulted his notes. 'Amaretto di Saronna: an Italian liqueur created in 1525 by a beautiful young widow.'

Parker whistled. 'Very Dilys Dayish!'

'I'll stand you one tonight, Parker, if said lady author didn't buy up the entire local stock. There were several cases of it in her cupboard.'

'Thanks, Sarge.'

'And just notice its bouquet. That's smell to you, Parker. A good masking aroma.'

'So you do think it's poison, do you, sir?'

'I think the butler did it,' quipped Sergeant Wellow.

'Oh, sir, that's too-too Dilys Dayish.'

Constable Parker read the autopsy and the lab reports, and reread them. Dilys Day had been poisoned. She'd died from a veterinary substance used to put down animals, but there were few hints as to how it had been administered. Constable Parker looked bemused.

'There's nothing. Nothing in the champagne, the glasses …'

'Remember the amaretto,' advised Sergeant Wellow.

'Nothing in that bottle either. Everything clean and wholesome.'

'But there were traces on her right hand,' said Sergeant Wellow. 'Minute traces on her thumb and index finger.'

'You mean suicide? She laced her own drink or something.'

'I think she did just that, Parker.'

'But why? She was rich and successful,' protested Parker, 'and she'd just started another book. It doesn't make sense.'

'Not suicide,' said Sergeant Wellow. 'I think she poisoned her drink unwittingly. And what's more, I think she had a higher opinion of we policemen than I gave her credit for.'

Dilys Day's household assembled in Mrs. Giles kitchen once more. They eyed each other suspiciously; Sergeant Wellow had announced one of them a murderer.

'Whoever poisoned your employer knew her habits very well.'

'That could be any one of us,' commented Jenkins.

'It could be,' replied Sergeant Wellow, 'but I think it was you, Jenkins.'

'Me?' the butler's voice remained calm. 'But I wasn't here.'

'It wasn't necessary for you to be here,' said Sergeant Wellow, patiently. 'The poison was in the crushed ice. The ice you, Jenkins, prepared to chill the champagne. You knew there was a more than even chance Miss Day would have an amaretto during the afternoon.'

'And she takes ice from the ice-bucket,' accused Mrs. Giles. 'I've seen her do it.'

'So have I,' cried Miss Fanshawe.

Jenkins darted for the door.

'Let him go,' said Sergeant Wellow. 'The boys outside will pick him up.'

Constable Parker sat at the bar of the station local and sipped amaretto on the rocks.

'So all Jenkins had to do on his return was slip into the study, flush the poisoned ice into the sewer, wash the glass and replace the ice-bucket.'

'And put the amaretto back in the cupboard,' added Sergeant Wellow. 'A bit of tidying up and he was rid of a boss who stole his ideas and paid him in favours instead of royalties.'

'You said the butler did it, sir. You said that from the beginning.'

'The ice was fresh. It had hardly melted although the study was warm. You should have noticed that, Parker.'

'Yes, sir.'

'And you should have noticed the clue Miss Day managed to type before she died. You noted its alliteration.'

'I thought that was the first line of a book, sir.'

'So did Jenkins, fortunately. It was a clue all right. Check your notes, Parker. It all adds up.' And Sergeant Wellow read from his own notebook: *It was a wet, windy Wednesday somewhere in the West Country. The champagne had been put on ice when …*

'So it does, sir,' agreed Parker. 'Still, it would make a good start to a story.'

'Yes,' sighed Sergeant Wellow, 'but it's what comes after the "when" that's difficult.'

'I'm sure you've got some notes there that would help you, sarge,' said Parker and sipped his amaretto. Its aroma was of almonds. Another case of alliteration.

ABOOROO'S CHOICE

I am Abooroo. The Reverend Mister Johnson has not changed my name.

The land has a new name. The names of hills and rivers are different, but I am always Abooroo.

'Do you live, Abooroo?' asks Nanbarry when we meet in the camp.

'Abooroo lives,' I say, 'and so does Nanbarry.'

But Nanbarry looks uncertain. The eyes of the dreamer are no longer wise and all knowing. He plucks at his new covering, fingers his hidden body to make certain he will become a man.

'You are Nanbarry,' I tell him. 'And I am Abooroo, given to you at birth.'

I was born as the morning star promised the return of our Mother Sun. As it told the world her kindling twigs would soon be lit, I was being given life. I gave my first cry along with the brown winged *goo-gaur-gaga*, who laughs aloud at every dawn to wake those still asleep. My father stirred up the fire to keep me warm and my mother gave me her breast. She carried me until I was able to walk and could follow the paths my family trod. I was given to Nanbarry but, before my bleeding came, I was taken to Mister Johnson's fire.

Nanbarry and I were gathering oysters near the rocks when the peeled people came. They broke into our world in great canoes. Strange shaped canoes as high as trees. Canoes without paddles yet, somehow, they flew over the water like clouds in the sky. I forgot my hunger.

'Look, Nanbarry, look.'

His face told me he had seen this in his dreaming.

Fishing stopped. The men hurried all the women and children back into the wood.

'Come, Abooroo.'

My mother snatched up her line and hooks and pushed me ahead. I ran on obediently, but then turned aside and hid myself. When everybody had gone to safety, I stepped back onto the path and returned to the fishing place. I was curious and so was Nanbarry.

He was there before me, at the place above the water where there was cover from the trees.

'You should be with your mother,' he said.

'So should you,' I answered.

'Go now.'

He pointed the way with his spear, but I did not obey. He was a wise one but not yet a man to beat me, and I did not want to return alone. My mother's anger would be less when she saw I'd been with Nanbarry.

Below us were the rocks and the scattering of oyster shells we had dropped. Beyond, my father and the other men splashed in the water raising their spears and shouting a warning.

'Warra! Warra!'

But the great canoes did not go away. They kept coming until they were more than the fingers on my hand.

'Are there giants in them?' I asked Nanbarry. 'Have you seen them?'

'Perhaps,' he said.

Mother Sun's fire burnt low in the sky and the strange canoes rested large on the water she had turned to flame. Unknown words, loud and harsh, like the call of the dingo, startled us. We fled to our mothers.

There were no giants. There were people. A different people.

'I did not say I saw giants,' said Nanbarry. 'But these peeled ones are like the spirits of the dead. They can become giants.'

They were peeled of colour as wood that is burnt to ash or oyster shells that whiten in the sun. But, unlike the spirits, the peeled people covered their bodies, hid themselves away in the colours of the birds and flowers. Our men were puzzled because they could not tell if they faced a man or a woman. They poked at the strangers until one cast off the covering, like a snake sheds its skin, while another pointed and chanted, 'Penis! Penis!'

A joyful shout of recognition went up from our men.

'Gadiay! Gadiay!'

They danced and flaunted their manhood and mimicked the peeled one's chant.

'Perhaps they are our ancestors,' I said to Nanbarry, for I'd heard my father say this of the peeled men. 'Come from the Dreamtime.'

'No,' said Nanbarry, 'they bring death.'

'Are you sure?'

'I have seen this,' he said. 'They bring death to many ... to Nanbarry ... and to Abooroo.'

'But Nanbarry,' I protested. 'They have given us fish.'

'And taken it,' he said. 'So many fish scooped out of the water. A giant's catch.'

I fell silent thinking of the giant creatures of the Dreamtime my father had told me about. The brothers Byama, who turned themselves into enormous kangaroos; the great frog who swallowed all the world's water and caused a drought; and the mighty Rainbow Serpent who arches his back in the sky when it rains.

Nanbarry touched my arm.

'Perhaps I woke before the dream ended.' He spoke gently. 'I am not fully formed in wisdom.'

'If they are not ancestors,' I said, echoing my father's voice, 'they will soon return to their own world for they have no women.'

But the peeled men did have women. I heard their

mating noise above the thunder. I saw them in the wood by the jagged light of the storm. Their bodies were covered and wet with rain, but I saw there were women when the peeled men tore away the coverings and used their gadiay as our men do. Some women fought and screamed, others lay laughing in the mud and took one man after another. As I watched their backs arch and hands clench, I thought of Nanbarry.

'They deceived us,' he raged. 'A few men became many, and now they have women. What else is hidden in the great canoes?'

Perhaps the mittayon was hidden for we did not see or hear it come ashore. But both Nanbarry and I felt its presence as our bodies began to ache and our mouths filled with sores. The family left us by the rocks, but now we were too weak and tired to search for oysters or pull the shells apart.

'This is my dream,' whispered Nanbarry before he slept.

I saw that his face was spotted the colour of blood and knew the dream was true. I reached out to him and then my own eyes fell shut.

I woke, but my eyes would not open. In the unsleeping dark I felt a swarm of insects beneath my skin, wriggling, twisting, trying to burst out. I wanted to scratch, scratch, scratch. Scratch my face. Scratch my arms. Scratch my legs. But I could not. My arms were tied. A piece of fish, warm and moist, was put to my lips and I took it into my mouth. There was laughter, womanly words and more fish. I knew I was with the peeled people. I knew that I would live. I wondered what had happened to Nanbarry.

The mittayon has eaten into more than Nanbarry's skin.

'You did see true things,' I tell him. 'But the goo-gaur-gaga laughed you awake before the dream ended. You told Abooroo this.'

Nanbarry picks at the scars on his arm and says nothing.

'The peeled people have helped us live,' I argue. 'You cannot give back anger.'

'Abooroo does not understand.' He speaks to the earth. 'I am angry because I am afraid.'

'Afraid?'

'I fear men who can change dreams.'

I am not afraid. I sit at the Reverend Mister Johnson's fire. I have shelter, warmth, food, and his woman has given me a covering.

'Dress,' says Mister Johnson.

'Dress,' I echo.

I like the feel of it on my skin and that it hides the marks of the mittayon.

'Smallpox,' says Mister Johnson, pointing to the bird beak scars.

'Mittayon'

He scratches on something with a feather.

'Mit-ta-yon.'

Mister Johnson is happy that I mimic his words: King George. By the grace of God. England. Lord Sydney. Convicts. Scum. Jesus Christ. Supplies.

He tells his woman that I am a clever girl and will be useful.

When my people are seen near the camp that is when I am useful. I tell them they will be well treated if they come in.

'Abooroo knows this is true.' I bare my mittayon scars. 'Show yours,' I urge Nanbarry, but he will not. He pulls his arm away in anger so that no-one listens to me.

'Never mind,' says Mister Johnson. 'Next time we'll come without him.'

He leaves bread and meat at the side of the path.

Nanbarry is like a bird that flies from tree to tree and cannot decide which has the best fruit. I often see him leave the camp and go into the woods. I know he sits naked by friendly fires and searches for the dreams he has lost. Then he covers himself and returns to feast on the peeled men's meat.

Everyday I eat and talk and learn with Mister Johnson. But now he talks of 'short rations' and 'prayers for a ship from England.' I do not have enough words to ask why his woman keeps the child in her belly if there is hunger, but I am happy that she does.

'I am to give the child a name,' I tell Nanbarry. 'Mister Johnson says it is Abooroo's choice.'

We are walking the path to the place where two men wait and watch for Mister Johnson's 'ship from England'. This is the edge of our world. An angry, noisy place where the mighty water does battle against the mighty rocks. Before the peeled people came we believed there was nothing but that mighty water beyond where Mother Sun wakes to bring us light. Now we know there are other people, other worlds.

'So why do they want ours?' asks Nanbarry.

'Perhaps they have been sent by our ancestors. To show us new ways.' I am thinking of Mister Johnson's garden and the names I echoed: grape, cucumber, pumpkin, potato.

'No.' Nanbarry's voice warns Abooroo like the voice of her father.

'But they are kind people.'

'Not all of them. Abooroo is a girl. She does not see everything.'

'And what has Nanbarry seen?

'I told you what I saw.' Nanbarry's eyes are bright. 'I see death.'

I want to challenge him – to say that I live, he lives – but I keep silent as we come to the look-out. Nanbarry has agreed to show the men here how we bury our dead and they are waiting for us, as well as for the ship from England.

Nanbarry scoops out a hollow in the earth and pushes in dry standing sticks around its edge. Then he goes to fetch branches from the trees. When he returns from the wood he is naked. He carries a shape like a body tied in a leafy bundle. He smiles at me as he places it in the prepared hollow. He covers it over with earth so that the sticks point out like thorns. Then he makes fire, which excites the look-out men to whistle and shout, and he sets the sticks aflame. As the fire crackles and the smoke rises, Nanbarry grabs at my hand and drags me away. I hear the men laughing.

'Let go,' I shout at Nanbarry, but he does not listen.

I struggle, but he is too strong. He has grown to manhood in the camp. I stumble after him down the steep path to the shore, along the sand and into a cave. I know the shape and smell of the place.

'This is where my family sleep.'

'Yes.' He lets me go. 'They do not come here since your friends brought the mittayon.'

'Mister Johnson says it was not in his ships.'

'We could not see it,' Nanbarry says as he builds a fire. 'So how do they? Have they better eyes?'

I think of the magic eye Mister Johnson showed me. He can make giants like in the Dreamtime. How I jumped when the little ant I could squash between my fingers became a monster. Nanbarry has lived in the camp and yet he sees only bad things for our people.

'Your father has not returned', he blows on the fire, 'so Abooroo must walk with me.'

As the fire makes flames, I see Nanbarry has spears lying ready and clay to smear on his body. I realise that the ceremony at the look-out was a true burial. His life with the peeled people is dead.

'You burnt your clothes.'

'Give me the dress,' he demands.

I clutch the dress to my body, suddenly afraid to be naked. Afraid of Nanbarry seeing that my breasts are beginning to swell and that my bleeding will come soon.

'Nanbarry,' I plead, pointing to the spears, 'this is not the way of a wise one.'

'I am not a dreamer now.' He grabs up a spear. 'The peeled ones are hungry, their men weak. We can drive them from our world.' He stirs the fire with the spear. 'Give me the dress.'

'No!'

My defiance echoes around us and startles Nanbarry.

'No ... o ... o ... o!

He lunges at me, but I am too quick and run from the cave. I hear a spear shiver into the sand beside me, but I do not stop. I do not stop.

I *am* Abooroo although I no longer walk naked. I *am* Abooroo although I do not sleep by the fire of my father or lie with Nanbarry. I nurse the Reverend Mister Johnson's child. I have given her my mother's name. She is Milbah. This is Abooroo's choice.

LUCKY JACK CASH

'Any you chaps know what a witch looks like?'

No answer. Only the slap, slap of the waves as we ride out the storm; the creak of hawsers holding ships row on row; the breath of men weary with waiting and too little sleep.

'Crikey, Corp,' says one, 'that's a damn fool question at a time like this.'

I know it's a damn fool question, but I persist.

'I mean a real witch. A living, breathing witch.'

'Are you telling us Jerry's got a broomstick brigade?'

Mrs Winter didn't have a broomstick. At least, I never saw one in her square, story-book house, the last on my list of 'possibles'.

'We're told you might have a spare room,' I said, 'just for a couple of weeks.'

'Then we're going home to get wed,' added Margy. 'Back up to Yorkshire.'

Give Mrs Winter her due, she never commented on Margy's condition.

'I'm told you're an army wife,' I said. 'You'll know how difficult it is to make personal arrangements in wartime.'

Mrs Winter never said, 'best not leave it much longer' like the others whose doors we'd knocked on. She put an arm round Margy and led her inside.

The men are laughing. A broomstick brigade!

'I've heard there's good witches,' I am serious, unsmiling. 'Ones that help people.'

'So how come we're stuck on a bleeding transport waiting for some freak storm to clear?'

The laughter dies.

' 'Cos Herr Hitler's got zee Valkyries.' The wag begins to lah-lah a tune. Repetitive. Threatening. He strikes an operatic pose. 'Vee 'ave ways of stopping zee invasion. Achtung flying broomsticks!'

The tune and the laughter rise again. The men begin to clap and stamp out the rhythm, to sing out the tune.

'Shut up! I order. 'Shut up!'

The performance stutters to a halt.

'Get your heads down and get some sleep.'

Men muttering, twitching, dreaming, dreading.

'You all right, Jack?'

Rory is concerned. He's a good mate. We've looked out to each other since '42.

'It's this delay. Waiting about. Gets everybody on edge.'

'Not like you, Jack.'

'No.'

'Not thinking about that Yorkshire lass?'

'No!'

'Funny how it turned out, tho'. You could have saved the cost of that telegram.'

'Leave it, Rory.'

'Mind, I thought she was a bit young for you.'

'Shut it, Private,' I snap, 'and get to sleep.'

I followed Margy into Mrs Winter's house. We sat at the kitchen table and drank cocoa.

'I'm used to sleeping rough,' I said, 'but you can see Margy needs a bed.'

'I've a room you can have for a couple of weeks,' said Mrs Winter.

'Oh,' the tears Margy had been holding back began to flow. 'We can't thank you enough.'

She hugged Mrs Winter. 'Jack and I are most grateful.'

'Yes,' I agreed. 'Most grateful.'

'The room is all I can afford,' said Mrs Winter. 'I'll have to charge for food. Has Margy got her ration book?'

Margy was wide-eyed, startled, like a child caught dipping damp fingers in the sugar bowl.

She shook her head.

'I'll take care of the grub,' I said quickly. 'I've a mate in the cookhouse. And there'll be a few extras for your trouble.'

Mrs Winter smiled.

'The rations don't go far these days,' she cleared away the cocoa cups, 'not with two young boys to feed.'

There aren't enough bunks for every man from our

hut, but Rory's marked out deck space with kitbags for those without. He should have got the stripes before me, but I've always been the lucky one. Lucky Jack Cash, that's me.

I lived up to my moniker the day I met Margy on the moor. She waved at the lorry and I slammed my foot on the brakes. She left off hefting sheep and came running. We sat on a dry-stone wall and smoked a Woodbine.

'Well, my lovely,' I said. 'I didn't expect to meet a beauty like you working up here.'

She blushed creamy pink and kicked her heels against the wall. She was young, barely out of school.

'My dad's the shepherd on Flinty's Farm. We live over Kimbleside.' She pointed away into the hazy distance.

'What's your name?' I asked.

'Margy. Margery Bates.'

'Corporal Jack Cash.' I took her hand. Soft, oiled with wool fat and smelly. 'Now we're officially introduced.'

I could have left it there and no harm done. A sturdy farm-girl with a whiff of rank mutton wasn't my usual style, but I sensed something wild and untamed in Margy, smelt her readiness as well as the sheep shit, and added, 'So I can come calling.'

'No, not at the farm, but I'm up here most days or I can cycle anywhere after work.'

I knew I was Margy's first, but there wasn't much I could teach her. She was a natural.

Lustful. Exuberant. Joyful. Loud. Better than any whore. I couldn't get enough of her – nor she of me – amid the flock grazing on the moor, in the back of the lorry or up against the wall of the barracks.

'Manoeuvres by day, manoeuvres by night.' Rory commented wryly.

But I didn't care. My khaki life had taken on colour. Margy's green eyes, hazelnut hair and freckled, sun-touched skin. I was having the time of my life. I knew it couldn't last.

'Good work, Rory.' I settle on the deck beside him. He doesn't answer. I kick his shin. 'I know you're not asleep.'

'So put me on a charge, Corporal!'

'I didn't mean to pull rank. Sorry.'

Rory sits up and offers me a Woodbine.

'What's bothering you, Jack? And don't say this hanging about. We're all in the same boat – literally.' He giggles at his own joke.

'I've a feeing,' I draw heavily on the fag, 'a bad feeling …'

'Shut that!' Rory interrupts. 'You're Lucky Jack Cash who always falls on his feet. Corporal 'Bloody Lucky' Cash! Hut D's talisman.' He kicks my shin. 'Now, who are you?'

'Lucky Jack Cash,' I answer. 'But …'

'No buts …'

'Rory, I need to know if a witch would have children.'

'For Christ's sake, Jack, don't lose it now.'

I wanted Margy to lose the baby. Nearly five months gone and I was so taken with her I hadn't noticed the missed periods, the thickening waistline, the talk of ewes dropping lambs.

'It's Nature, Jack. It's what happens.'

I plied her with gin, told her to take hot baths, handled her roughly. Nothing worked.

'I'm sixteen in two months.' Margy was radiant. 'We could get married then.'

'Right,' I said, 'consider yourself engaged.'

'Oh, Jack.' She flung her arms around my neck. 'I do love you so.'

I took her in the back of the lorry. After all, the damage was done and there was a war on.

A month later the war took my unit south to Hampshire. I hadn't reckoned on it taking Margy as well. Rory and I were unloading the lorry when he grabbed his rifle and indicated for me to throw back a tarpaulin. There, between the boxes of ammuni-tion, sat Margy, cramped and uncomfortable.

'Jesus Christ, Margy! You could have got yourself shot. What are you doing here?'

'Don't be cross, Jack.'

'I told you I'd write –'

'But I couldn't bear for us to be apart.'

'Get her out of here,' said Rory. 'Find some digs in the village.'

Margie and Mrs Winter got on just fine.

'She's like a big sister to me,' said Margy, 'and her boys call me aunty.'

But Mrs Winter took against me for some reason. There weren't that many extras from the cookhouse, or perhaps we outstayed our welcome as two weeks stretched into four, but like I told her, 'You can't odds the Army. You should know that. I'll take Margy home as soon as I get leave.'

I fancied she resented the nights I spent under her roof. A mature woman, no husband to hand, lying in a double bed listening to me and Margy, picturing us beyond the wooden partition, of course she was jealous. Mind, Margy was less enthusiastic now, always complaining she was tired. So, I let her sleep a bit and then went about persuading her.

One morning Mrs Winter waylaid me as I left Margy's bed to return to duty.

'Up early today, Missus,' I joked.

'Corporal Cash ...'

The formality was ominous.

'While Margy's under my roof I feel responsible.'

Oh, spare me the big sister act!

'So,' she continued. 'I don't want her being pestered. She's pregnant ...'

The Cashes don't go round shooting blanks!

'And if she says, "No" – well, you should be a gentleman and desist.'

Desist! Jealous cow! Want some for yourself?

'Think what you like, Jack Cash …'

Had she read my mind?

'But if you hurt Margy, believe me, you won't be calling yourself lucky ever again.'

Interfering old witch! I put in for leave as soon as I got back to camp.

'Listen, Jack.' Rory lights me another fag. 'We're all scared shitless and this silly talk isn't helping. Now's the time you gotta earn those stripes'

'I've a bad feeling –'

'That's guilt.' Rory grips my arm. 'Guilt. Nothing more. You feel bad about Margy.'

'I couldn't marry her.'

'Not with a wife and two nippers, you couldn't,' Rory snorts. 'That's why I sent the telegram. Remember?'

I got my leave and we said goodbye to Mrs Winter.

'Think about us Thursday week,' said a tearful Margy. 'We're getting married by special licence.'

Margy and I took the train north. Rory's telegram arrived the day after we'd booked into the hotel near home barracks.

'Sorry, Margy. I've got to report back immediately.'

Her face paled. She clutched at her huge belly.

'Can't odds the Army.' I waved the telegram at her. 'It's damned bad luck, happens all the time in war.'

'But what am I going to do?'

'Go home. It's not far.' I gave her what money I had. 'I'll come for you when it's all over.'

I left her weeping on the bed. The bell-boy was in the passage.

'Telegram, Corporal Cash.'

This time my re-call was official.

'So, you could have saved your money and my time on the telegram,' Rory stubs out his fag. 'That doesn't make Mrs Winter a witch.'

'But don't you see,' I argue, 'my excuse, the telegram lie, it all came true. '

'Of course it did.' Rory stifles a yawn. 'You're Lucky Jack Cash. You always fall on your feet.'

His eyes close.

I do not sleep. I hear the judder of engines firing up below and the busyness of sailors as they cast off. I try to think of the drill for the landing craft, to visualise the landmarks on the map, to recall our objectives. I remember only my last meeting with Mrs Winter.

My lorry was waiting in convoy as we left for embarkation and there she stood, watching history with her two small boys.

'Jack!' She ran to the cab. 'How did the wedding go?'

'Wonderful. The sun shone. Margy looked beautiful.'

'You're a liar Jack Cash. I've heard the talk and I won't wish you good luck. I just wish you everything that you've wished yourself.'

Her threat the morning I'd labelled her a witch echoed and re-echoed inside my head.

'Not long now,' says Rory. 'Stay close.'

'Stay close,' I parrot belatedly

The men from Hut D gather round their talisman. My thoughts gather on a letter back at camp addressed to *Miss Margery Bates.* I paid for the writing and for it to be posted at the end of June. In neat script, it tells Margy how the writer tended me as I lay mortally wounded on the invasion beach and that my dying thoughts were of her and the baby.

In a few moments, when we touch France and the ramp goes down, I shall know if Mrs Winter is a real witch and if I'm still Lucky Jack Cash.

THE ASH BUSH SPIES

Alan and I spent hours playing in the misnamed ash bush. The slope of the garden and Grandfather's seat let us step, rather than climb, into its branches. It was from the ash bush that I set out to save the world. I was eight and a bit when I saved Lena, although my concern was for Alan at the time.

Mother told us that in Grandfather's day the ash was cut back regularly and the seat he'd fixed to its trunk was varnished, but she had more than enough to do and no money to spare for such things. So the bush tried to become the tree it was meant to be and now new, grey-green growth encircled the cropped branches. It resembled an untidy clump of basket frames in which we could sit unseen by those coming and going in the narrow lane below.

Grandfather's seat was shabby but still held firm and we made easy escape into our watch-tower or, more often, to the cock-pit of a Spitfire from which we continued the war long after the victory flags were packed away.

'This is Red Leader. This is Red Leader. Keep your eyes skinned. They'll come at you from out of the sun.'

'You can't be leader,' complained my brother. 'Girls don't fly Spitfires.'

I ignored him.

'Bandits at two o'clock. Two o'clock. Tally-ho! Aka … aka … aka …'

'Girls don't fight wars,' insisted Alan.

I could fight anybody.

'Make the noises,' I ordered as I hit him. 'That's all boys are any good at.'

Alan made a noise. He went blubbering to Mother.

'Audrey!' Mother's voice demanded obedience. 'Come here this minute.'

I clambered down from the cockpit, tossed aside my flying jacket and reported in.

Do your worst. You won't make me talk. I shall never betray my country.

'Take that look off your face, my girl,' said Mother. 'Just 'cos your father's gone don't mean you can run riot.'

I wasn't running riot. I was saving the world. And anyway, Father had never been around.

He was a snapshot photograph. He was the stranger who turned up during the flag waving. The stranger who disrupted our routine, intruded on our closeness and caused havoc in our lives. That's why we'd come to live in grandfather's old cottage.

The best game in Ash Bush was spying. Hidden high above the lane, Alan and I kept watch on the neighbours and eavesdropped on their conversation. There was Aunt Lil, in her long skirt and Mother Riley hat, going to town for her daily quartern of gin. There were the Tenderfoot Twins, bleached hair and high heels, tottering to mysterious assignations. And there was Lena who kept house for her father and rouged her face as she walked below us.

'That Lena's growing up too fast,' said Mother. 'Needs a firmer hand, she does.'

We were wizard spies, Alan and I. We were on to Charlie Morgan days before Mother noticed anything.

'What's he doing round here?' she asked. 'That's twice this week I've seen him hanging about on the bridge.'

Careless Talk Costs Lives! Keep Mum!

'Perhaps he's fishing,' I said.

Mother laughed. A short, brittle, ha-ha sort of laugh.

'He's always fishing, that one.'

I knew Charlie wasn't catching tiddlers because Alan and I were in ash bush when he swaggered up the lane from the river. He stopped right below us, lit up a cigarette – Charlie always had cigarettes – and tried to blow smoke rings. We stared at the top of his head, all Brylcreem and comb marks, and hardly dare breathe. Charlie Morgan wouldn't take kindly to spies. I wasn't scared for myself.

Come on, Charlie. We've had a tail on you. Where 'd you get the fags? Fell off the back of a lorry, did they?

But I had to think of Alan – younger, frailer, and intent on watching the strands of smoke drift upward into the slender leaves. I mouthed a silent prayer that Charlie wouldn't blow a perfect ring that had to be admired until, wavering and disintegrating, it pointed us out.

Hellfire! The searchlight's got us. Make a run for it chaps.

My prayer was answered. Charlie stamped out his fag, leant against our garden wall – legs crossed, hands in his pockets – and just waited. This was important. Charlie Morgan never hung around without reason. Suddenly, he spoke.

'About time too. I were just about to get going.'

Lena was coming down the lane. She stopped and smiled at Charlie.

'Me old man was late away to the allotment. I had to clear away tea things.'

'D'you want a fag?' asked Charlie.

'Don't mind,' said Lena.

We watched as Charlie lit up two cigarettes.

'Here's looking at you, kid!' Charlie handed Lena a fag.

'Thanks, Charlie. I loved that film.'

They stood close together. Charlie's dark, greasy hair next to Lena's which was copper coloured and shiny as if it had just been given a vinegar rinse.

'Wanna see a smoke ring?' asked Charlie.

'Don't mind,' said Lena.

Charlie took a drag and puffed his cheeks like a plump pigeon but, before he could blow, we heard Aunt Lil bidding farewell to her companion cat as she set off for the *Jug and Bottle.* Lena fled.

'Charlie ran, too,' I reminded Alan, 'He legged it before Aunt Lil got down her steps.' Charlie Morgan, who boasted he wasn't a conchie, who swore he'd have made a difference if he'd been in uniform, that Charlie Morgan had run.

'He ran,' I repeated, 'and from Aunt Lil of all people. He's got to be up to something.'

'I reckon Mum's right,' said Alan, 'He's a no-good townie.'

'A spiv,' I added, 'who goes to the black market for cigarettes and stockings.'

'He must hide the stuff somewhere,' said Alan.

'If we could find it, they might give us a medal.'

I badly wanted a medal like the one Father had given Alan before he upped and left us.

I kept the record of our spying in a red exercise book. I'd chosen red for danger and written 'TOP SECRET. KEEP OUT' on the cover. I prised it from behind the chest that separated our beds and started a clean page for Charlie and Lena.

It wasn't long before the Tenderfoot Twins proved us

right about Charlie. Neither he nor Lena worried at their approach.

'Well, Charlie,' the sisters chorused, 'fancy bumping into you … and lovely Lena, looking all grown up.'

'I am grown up,' said Lena,

'Of course you are, dear, and you deserve some fun'. They giggled. 'And Charlie knows how to have fun, don't you, Charlie?'

'All right, all right,' said Charlie. 'That's enough.' He pulled stockings from the inside pocket of his jacket.

'Nylons!' shrieked the twins. Each grabbed a pair and held them up to the light. 'What a darling, darling man. You hang on to him, Lena.'

'I mean to,' said Lena.

'And don't worry,' the two chimed together like clocks on the hour. 'Your secret's safe with us.'

Thought you'd never be found out; did you, Charlie? Dashed clever, I grant you, but not quite clever enough. You might as well come clean because we know your secret, and we're going to find where you hide the stockings.

Friday was Mother's night out and Aunt Lil came to sit in our parlour and drink dandelion wine instead of gin. Mother always made a point of seeing her home. I'd listen for them going past our bedroom window. The old woman complaining she could manage. Mother insisting on her neighbourly duty. That's how I heard them worrying over Lena.

'A girl Lena's age needs talking to,' said Mother.

'Happen he has.' Aunt Lil's stick tip-tapped unsteadily down the path.

'I doubt it,' said Mother. 'He gives more time to potatoes and cabbages than bringing up his daughter.'

'Don't interfere,' advised Aunt Lil. 'His sort won't thank you.'

'But she needs to know the danger ...' Mother's voice grew faint, but I heard that red word: danger. I fell asleep knowing the Ash Bush Spies had to keep a special watch on Lena.

We watched Lena whenever possible. Lena doing the chores; outside beating the mats, hanging the washing, feeding the hens. And Lena meeting Charlie by the ash bush. Then she was like a summer flower, growing bolder and brighter by the minute. Her drab don't-show-the-dirt dress was swopped for a riot of rainbow colours, all tucked and shaped and buttoned with pearls. She looked like a film star.

'Me old man would kill me,' she laughingly told Charlie. 'This were me Mam's. I found a caseful in the attic.'

'Yer old man's a fool. You should have nice things. Lots of nice things. Let me talk to him.'

'No, Charlie. Not yet.'

'There is a way.' Charlie drew Lena close and whispered in her ear.

'Charlie!'

'Why not? You don't want to be at his beck and call all yer life'

Lena made no reply. Charlie kicked our wall.

'I'm walking you home. I ain't afraid of him.'

We were having supper when we heard Charlie whistling his way back. There had been no face-to-face with Lena's father; he worked till dusk on his allotment.

Don't pretend you didn't know that, Charlie. Everybody knows Lena's dad is wed to his allotment. You got a big mouth, Charlie, but we know what you are. We seen you. You're a runner.

When Alan and I grew bored with spying and hunting the stash of stockings, we went fishing. We were downstream, jam-jars poised, when I looked up from the water and saw Lena hurrying over the bridge and following the path upstream.

'What a bit of luck,' I exclaimed. 'She didn't see us. Come on.'

Lena quickened her pace. We held back. She met Charlie at the stile. We flopped into the long grass and lay still. When we looked up, they had gone. I led the way to the stile and pointed to a trail of trampled grass.

'Stockings,' I whispered. 'Follow me.'

They were lying in an alcove in the hedge. Lena, skirt adrift, legs sprawled. Charlie was leaning over her –

kissing, touching, commanding. A snatch of song from the senior playground echoed in my head.

It's only human nature after all, To take a pretty girlie by the wall, To pull down her protections, And fiddle with her …

I sensed the danger. This was something my little brother should not see.

'Get off her, you big bully,' I shouted. 'Leave her alone.'

Lena screamed. Charlie rolled aside, fumbling, face all flushed.

'Little buggers,' he roared. 'Little buggers, I'll get you for this.'

We ran like mad and so did Charlie.

He would have caught us if Mother had not been on the bridge. She was dressed up, hair crimped and curled, calling us to bed. I'd forgotten it was Friday. We clung to her. Breathless. Tearful. Telling tales. Lena clung to Charlie in the same state.

'Nothing happened,' she sobbed. 'Nothing happened.'

'Home, Audrey,' ordered Mother, 'and straight to bed. Aunt Lil's waiting.'

Later I heard Mother helping Aunt Lil home. They'd both been on the dandelion wine.

'I'll stand before my Maker a virgin,' lisped Aunt Lil. 'No man has touched my lily white thighs.'

'Best way,' said Mother. 'Men! My kids save his daughter …'

'From a fate worse than death,' interrupted Aunt Lil.

'They save his daughter,' repeated Mother. 'And what thanks do they get?'

I dreamt about my medal.

But I was an unsung heroine. No-one, not even Lena, said thank-you. Her father thrashed Charlie good and proper and then stoked a victory bonfire on his allotment. The rainbow colours – red, yellow, blue and green, – curled into flame. The pearl buttons cracked and popped. Charlie did a runner and Lena no longer rouged her face as she walked beneath the ash bush.

SMOOTHING IRONS

Mother is set to do the ironing. The ironing. Not the quick once over she gives my vest and liberty bodice, but the ironing for J.J. Walton and Company.

She irons at the kitchen table, the extra leaf pulled out and steadied on its foldaway leg. She spreads an old blanket and then a clean sheet to protect the table's oil-cloth and smooths out the creases with the flat of her hand.

The real flat-iron is heating on the gas stove.

'Watch yourself, Maddie,' says Mother, 'I've got more than enough to look out to.'

I know not to stand too close when the burner is alight and sizzing. I know, because once I bent to study the burst of blue-gold flame. I watched it curling up from beneath the black, blunted arrow of the iron and singed my hair. I remember a smell of homemade brittle toffee and Mother roughly shoving me aside and pushing my head under the tap.

'For God's sake, child,' she screamed, 'can't you keep still for one minute?'

And I screamed from the shock of the cold water running over my head, down my neck and under my collar. Then Mother was holding me close.

'There, there, there.' She rocked me to and fro. 'You're all right now, Maddie. You're all right.'

'I'm wet,' I wailed. 'Right down to my vest.'

'So am I,' laughed Mother.

My dripping hair had left damp patches on her blouse where she'd hugged me close.

We dried our clothes and ourselves in front of the black-leaded range. My dress, vest and liberty bodice hung on the clothes horse alongside Mother's blouse.

'Maddie, Maddie, Head in the Clouds!' said Mother. 'What am I going to do with you?' She began snipping at my hair with her sharp cutting-out scissors. 'I have to work, Maddie, to feed you and Jamie. The bit of money your father sends goes nowhere.'

I knew it went in the cocoa tin on the mantelshelf, but I kept silent and watched my burnt hair fall to the floor.

'And when I'm working I need you to watch yourself and watch Jamie for me once school's out. I can't be doing both.'

She kept snipping and the hair kept falling. Hair all frizzed and welded at the ends like corn stubble after firing.

'We're on our own now, Maddie, just the three of us. I'm lucky to be able to work at home, but I need you to help not hinder. Piece-work only pays if I'm quick and get the job done on time.'

She swept up the ends of hair and threw them on the fire. They were gone in a terrifying flash of sudden flame.

So I look out to Jamie and he hates me for it.

'I want to go with the others,' he grizzles as I drag him back from school.

The big boys are off to the river to catch bubbleheads and minnows. They'll bring them to school in jam jars for the tomorrow's Nature lesson.

'You're too little,' I answer. 'You'd fall in.'

'Wouldn't! Wouldn't! Wouldn't!' Jamie scuffs to a halt. 'I want to go fishing.'

'Not today, Jamie.' I try to be patient. 'Mother's busy. J.J. Walton comes in the morning.' And I yank him home bit by bit like a farm-hand shifts an awkward, stubborn calf.

Every week J.J. Walton and Company bring Mother materials and measurements and she turns them into curtains, or bedspreads, or loose covers and cushions for easy chairs, sofas and settees. She 'makes up' for the soft furnishing department.

Hunched over the Singer sewing-machine, her feet working the treadle, Mother urges plains and patterns under the needle, swathes yards of piping cord to match or contrast and sews every cut piece into place. Her left hand flat behind the needle-foot, her right in front, she keeps the material taunt, the line of stitches straight. The faster she can work the treadle, the faster the needle forms the stitches. Up and down press Mother's feet, up and down goes the needle. Up and down whirring seams together, backs to sides, sides to fronts, arms to seats, edges piped, pelmets frilled or pleated.

This week's delivery is a rush job. A bolt of red roses, forever climbing and entwining and with its own flock of bluebirds flying from bud to leaf and back again.

'It's for a very good customer,' said J.J. Walton's man when he called. 'We don't want to let him down.'

'But this will take some matching,' said Mother, warily. 'Florals always do, let alone with birds.'

'A valued customer,' continued the company man. 'An account we can't afford to lose.' He pressed the cloth on Mother. 'There'll be a bonus if you complete on time. You can do with a bit extra, I'm sure. Things being the way they are.'

And Mother agreed.

I love to watch Mother work. She is an artist. One press upon the treadle and a severed rose rejoins its stem. Whirr, whirr and a bird's blue wing is mended.

'Look at this, Maddie. Such lovely colour.' She knots off the neatly stitched wing. 'The bluebird of happiness. It almost looks real.'

I touch the blue feathers, gently stroke the mended wing and wish that the bird was real.

'Nearly there, Maddie. Just the ironing and we're done.'

The ironing. When J.J. Walton calls tomorrow the covers and cushions for the valued customer's three-piece-suite will be pressed, folded and ready for delivery. And Mother will be a different person. Softer. Prettier. Happier. Perhaps we'll take Jamie fishing before she starts on the lot J.J. Walton leaves behind.

'Bit of good material this,' says Mother. 'Feel the weight.'

She gives me a chair cover to carry to the kitchen. The bluebirds and roses are heavy.

'Years of wear in it.' Mother follows with the matching cover. 'You don't get this quality off a market stall. What it is to have money!'

Mother is set to do the ironing. I hand her the iron-holder I'd made in needlework and she smiles at the stitching.

'Coming on, Maddie. Coming on.'

She picks up the flat-iron that is heating on the gas stove, spits on her first finger and dabs the bottom of the iron quickly as if to say, 'Burn me if you dare'. The spit sizzles furiously and she is satisfied. The iron is up to heat.

Mother uses that hot iron while a second is heating. She switches from one to the other pressing out her working creases under a clean, damp tea-towel, pressing in the box-pleats round the hem. Her face shines in the gentle steam.

'Comes up lovely,' she says. 'You can't beat working with good stuff.'

She folds the cover in its J.J.Walton tissue paper and starts on the second.

'Go see Jamie's asleep, there's a good girl.'

I climb the narrow stairs to our room and tip-toe in. But Jamie's bed is empty. Empty! His bread and jam untouched.

'He'll fall in,' I scream. 'He'll drown. He'll drown.'

Mother comes running, grabs my shoulders and shakes me hard.

'Where is he? I thought I told you to put him to bed.'

'It's not my fault,' I shout back. 'Why do I have to see to him? I'm not his mother.'

She slaps me so swiftly I don't see the blow coming, so hard my cheek stings. 'I hate you,' I sob. 'I hate you both. I hope he does drown.'

I want to say I'm sorry, say I didn't mean it, but there's no time because of the smell.

'Oh, my God!' Mother slaps her own face. 'You stupid woman, you.'

And she's away downstairs. I remember my singed hair. I know the bluebird's feathers are burning.

Mother snatches up the iron and clangs it down on the stove. She's too late. In the seat of the cover is a scorched silhouette, deep brown and black edged like burnt toast.

'What will J.J. Walton say?' I ask aghast.

'Bugger J.J. Walton,' says Mother. 'Let's find Jamie first.'

We run toward the river.

'Please, God. Please, God,' mutters Mother and I echo her.

'Please, God. I didn't mean it.'

At the stile we meet Jamie coming home with the other boys. He has a jam-jar complete with a string handle, minnows and water-weed. He holds it up for Mother to see and to stave off any scolding or embarrassing embrace. He's sturdy, defiant, one of the gang.

Mother puts us both to bed. Jamie's jar of minnows stands by his bed and he feeds them bits of his bread and jam.

'I'm sorry,' I whisper as she tucks me in. 'I didn't mean the things I said.'

'I know, Maddie. And I'm sorry, too. Will you forgive me?'

I hug her close and she hugs me back. Of course I forgive her anything, but will J.J. Walton and Company?

'What'll happen? What are you going to do? The van'll be here in the morning.'

'Don't worry your pretty little head about that.' She kisses me good-night. 'Sleep well now, Maddie. There's school tomorrow.'

In the morning the kitchen is strangely warm. There's

no bread or milk set ready for breakfast. The table is still covered with the sheet and blanket. The flat-irons stand upright on top the stove. I spit on my first finger and dab quickly against the smooth wedge of first one and then the other. There is no satisfying sizzle but the spit soon dries.

In the front room the gas-light is on and the curtains closed. But the Singer is open and threaded up. Snippets of blue Silko lie on the floor. On the table where Mother does the cutting out is the set of loose covers. Pressed, folded and ready for collection. I peep beneath the tissue paper. There is no scorch mark anywhere. Mother has mended the bluebirds and roses. She is asleep in the corner chair, my iron-holder in her lap. Very quietly I turn out the gas-light.

I tidy the kitchen and get Jamie his breakfast. I tell him if he doesn't wake Mother he can go to school on his own.

'Take your minnows,' I remind him, 'and tell Miss I'll be late today.'

He goes out the door as proud as a louse. I sit at the window and watch the road. I'm going to wait for J.J. Walton's van.

DIVE

He would make the dive tomorrow. Yes, tomorrow. He would be brave and ignore the concerns of his mother and Oma.

'You keep away from the dam, Rudi. It is not a good place. There are the ghosts of many souls beneath the water.'

'Yes, Oma, you told me.'

'I tell you again.' His grandmother gripped the arms of her high-backed chair and pulled her spine and shoulders halfway straight. 'And you, Rudi, must listen.' Her thin-as-a-thread voice thickened and her tired eyes brightened in anger. 'Keep away. The dam is bad luck for us. It is forbidden.'

Ten. Rudi counted ten brown blotches on Oma's right hand. It was a game he played when she forbade him the dam. How many ageing freckles before Oma loosened her grip and slumped back in the chair? Her skin was like paper left too long in the cold and damp of an attic. Mottled, musty and thin enough to give away the secrets it enwrapped. Grey-blue knots of veins and lumpy knuckles. No other boy in school had a grandmother as old as Rudi's.

'He won't go near the dam,' said his mother. 'Rudi's a good boy.'

Rudi did not want to be a good boy. He wanted to be one of 'those dam boys.' He wanted to be a member of the gang. One of the elite who was man enough to ignore the worry-bead restrictions imposed by the women of his house. But his classmates closed ranks against him. He was uninitiated.

'You know what you gotta do, Rudi.'

'And we've got to see you do it, or it don't count.'

'He ain't up to a dive. He's a mummy's boy. A baby.'

Rudi, head down, turned away and walked the white line of the playground's all-purpose pitch as if it was a precipice. How could he explain that he felt much older than his fourteen years and seven months? His home, music and books, his knowledge and his history were all dated, trapped in the time warp that was Oma and a widowed mother the age of most grandmothers.

'You were an autumn fruit,' she explained, 'like the grapes that make good wine. A late gift to comfort my old age.'

The boys at school sniggered.

'They thought they were safe and got caught out, and the effort did for your old man.'

It was true that Rudi could never remember his father in robust health.

A series of young men who came courting his older sister had stood in for him occasionally. They kicked a ball about and taught Rudi to swim, but he sensed they weren't really interested in little brother. Their motives were skewed toward getting a favour from Ilsa. Now he had two nieces not much younger than himself.

'Uncle Rudi,' taunted the other boys.

'Don't call me that.'

'Uncle Rudi,' echoed his nieces. 'Why haven't you made the dive?'

'The young today know nothing,' stormed Oma. 'Don't you and your man teach them right, Ilsa? You let your girls play on a grave?'

'Oma!' Ilsa reddened. 'It's different now. The dam is a nice place. Many people come to admire it.'

'Uncle Rudi hasn't dived,' chanted the nieces.

'But I will,' said Rudi, hastily.

'When? When?'

'No!' Oma clutched at her chair. 'No, Rudi. You promised.'

The gang sniggered louder, pointed and jeered. Rudi wasn't just a mummy's boy but Oma's as well. A goody-two-shoes who wouldn't take them off and stand barefoot on the parapet of the dam. Rudi wasn't only scared of the dive; he was scared of his grandmother. I hate her, thought Rudi. Why doesn't she die like other old women?

'I'll talk to my two,' said Ilsa. 'It's not right they torment you.'

'No,' said Rudi. 'That'll only make things worse.'

'You must understand Oma's concern, Rudi. You are the only boy in the family and so much like our granddad.'

Rudi nodded. Even Oma, when she was tired and confused, muddled the photographs of himself and grandfather. It was an easy mistake. Both were round faced, dark-eyed, full lipped and with the same broad forehead half-hidden by a mass of brown curls which refused to behave as mature hair should. Clipped short to celebrate the first pair of long trousers, the curls still asserted themselves and clung to the scalp in tight whirls. But there were no photographs of grandfather in middle-age or growing old. Rudi tried to imagine him with grey wayward hair and skin like Oma's.

'She blames the dam,' continued Ilsa. 'If there'd still been villages, houses, churches, the monastery. If there'd been no water. You know how she is.'

'There is water,' said Rudi, 'and I have to dive.'

'Can't you wait till …' Ilsa's voice trailed away.

'She isn't going to die,' snapped Rudi. 'She's going to live till I'm too old to dive.'

'Rudi!' Ilsa smiled in spite of herself. 'The dam was a great tragedy in Oma's life. To be widowed so young and her husband not to know about his baby.'

'Then I'll go and tell him.' Rudi was defiant. 'Tomorrow.'

Oma and his mother had always hated the dam, but Rudi had loved it once.

It was the place where his father's infirmity hadn't counted. Where they could be like any other father and son, walking hand-in-hand and taking patriotic pride in 'the edifice of the century'. Six years in the building and employing over a thousand labourers, the dam rose forty-seven metres in height and gently curved across the valley for four hundred metres. Rudi remembered his father reciting the statistics and showing him the workhouse where giant engines generated electricity. He felt again his father's grip on his coat as he leant over the parapet to watch winter floodwater gushing from the sluice gates. But when father died Oma took charge and the dam was forbidden.

'That water has had one of this family, I don't want it to claim another.'

Her superstitious fear had been drip-fed into her daughter and their double helping of worry eroded Rudi's pride and pleasure in the dam. The sea of water it contained became a constant threat, a fearful thing, a catastrophe in waiting, as Oma told and re-told how it had been for grandfather.

'What chance did he have against all that? So deep. So strong and angry, like some pent up animal let loose.'

Rudi saw his own face beneath the water, his curls swirling back and forth.

'When they brought him back I barely recognised him. He'd been in the water for days and knocked about so. But I knew those curls.' Oma smiled at her grandson. 'You've got his curls.'

Rudi worried about having a drowned man's hair. Perhaps it was an omen.

'I won't go near that water, Oma. I promise, promise, promise.'

Rudi now regretted that promise. It wasn't fair that he should be held to a childish vow. Oma's story became a bore. He began to count her age-spots and answer back. When his mother remonstrated with him, he shouted, 'I wish Papa was here.'

He saw the blank look of hurt in her eyes. He hadn't said, 'And not you', but he'd meant it and his mother understood.

'And I wish your papa was here, Rudi.' She fingered her wedding ring. 'It's not easy on my own.'

'He,' Rudi emphasised the word, 'wasn't afraid of the dam.'

'No,' said his mother, 'the water hadn't taken his father.'

'Oh, Mama, I'm sorry.' Rudi was shamefaced. 'I just don't want to be scared all my life.'

And he was afraid. The dive was nothing like going in off the board at the swimming pool, but it had to be faced, or in his adult life – at work, in church or down the pub – Rudi saw he'd be joshed forever as the one who hadn't dived.

He told his mother he was meeting friends at the swimming pool and rolled up his trunks and towel in front of Oma so that she had no reason to think he was being secretive. But once out of sight of the house, Rudi turned his bicycle toward the valley dam. Freewheeling down the road that descended the wooded hillside, whizzing past the jam of tourist cars, catching the scent of pine and wild lupin and the occasional glimpse of distant water, he let out long whoops of excitement.

'Jaaaaaa ... wooooh!.'

He was flying. He could almost forget his disappointment that Oma had not passed away in her sleep thus releasing him from the fearful need to break his promise.

Then abruptly he was out of the forest shadow. He slowed and dismounted. The brightness of sun on water. The reservoir lake! So close and so alive. Laughter from a couple on a pedalo, the shout of a successful fisherman, the distant chug of outboard motor, the smack of wind into canvas as sailing boats tacked about. From the top of the hill all had been silent and the boats so small they looked like toys in a bathtub. Now Rudi could see the identifying numbers on each sail and the summer colours of the crew. This was now. He wanted to belong. He turned his bike toward the dam.

'Well, look who's been let off his lead.'

'What you doing here, Rudi?'

'I'm going to dive.'

'Yeah, yeah! Taking your bike with you?'

Rudi blushed. The camp followers giggled.

'Dive, man, dive. We ain't stoppin' you.'

Rudi went to park his bike and get changed. The gang sprawled on a corner of sand the boys regarded as their patch. Here the narrow strand abutted the curve of the dam and a gentle slope made it easy to wade ashore after a dive. High above, clusters of tourists, lone day-trippers, couples or family groups, started or finished their promenade from one side of the valley to the other. They stopped to watch, take photographs or reward a good dive with coins thrown onto the sand.

'Go for it, Rudi. If you dare.'

He stood barefoot on the parapet.

'Dare you! Dare you!'

Rudi's toes gripped the edge. He looked down. So far and so deep. Deep enough to drown whole villages and cover church steeples. He heard Oma's voice.

'Water has a mind of its own. Anything, or anybody, that gets in its way is swept aside.'

He relaxed his toes and stepped back. Perhaps there was a better spot further along.

'Dive, Rudi. Dive.'

He waved to the gang and moved to the edge again. He wouldn't look down. He kept his gaze fixed on the grey roofed castle of Waldeck atop the opposite hill. He curled his toes over the rim of the coping stone and raised his arms. He heard cameras click and a buzz of foreign chatter, but then Oma whispered, 'Water does horrible things to a body. Sick with shock I was, for weeks, and crying so because he drowned thinking I was barren.'

Rudi let his arms fall to his side. The tourists moved on across the dam to the souvenir shops or the water park.

'Give it up, Rudi. You wanker!'

'You ain't going to dive.'

Rudi blinked away tears but stayed put. He looked up the valley, across the water. It seemed to darken with his concentration, the surrounding hills stood out in silhouette as the light faded. A clear, quiet summer night. Then the steady drone and dark shape of a plane flying very low. A Lancaster bomber banking slowly beneath the medieval walls of Waldeck castle … and another … then a third … and a fourth. The deafening throb of propeller engines, spotlights on the water, the spit of gunfire from the plane's front turret raking around him.

'Dive, Rudi. Dive for cover.'

He launched himself into the Eder. A rush of air and then the shock of water. Cold, dark and turbulent. A strong current dragged him down, down, sucking him toward the wall. A valley full of water was leaching away. Rudi thought his lungs would burst. He knew he was going to drown and now he knew why Oma wanted to live. Then, through the murk a mirror image of himself, curls swirling, reached out to help: Grandfather, in his Wehrmacht uniform, smiling at him and guiding him to the surface.

The gang were on their feet cheering as Rudi swam ashore.

'Great dive, Rudi.'

'But man, you had us worried there.'

'Where'd you learn to hold your breath like that?'

Rudi towelled himself dry. He was going home. He had something important to tell Oma.

SUNDAY BEST

Jonah awoke. His pillow was wet again. Dribble. His dribble. He turned the pillow, hid the damp patch against the bolster and lay on his back. Now the wayward spittle could not escape.

It was early. First light. How long before the knocker-up came tap-tapping at the window with his wake-up pole? Jonah listened. Silence in the street but sounds within his ears. Deep within. Raging water. The buzz of angry bees. Had he missed the wake-up signal? Was Mr. Briggs, pen poised, about to mark his name? Jonah Webb – docked one quarter.

'No, Mr. Briggs. Wait!' Jonah threw back the bed-covers. 'I'll be there before the shed door shuts.'

'Jonah?' Esther was awake. 'What are you looking for, Jonah?'

He'd not meant to disturb her but he couldn't find his breeches. Old man Briggs was a cunning fox. Like that red thief he walked abroad in the middle of the night. He'd stolen the breeches while they slept so he might make that mark: Jonah Webb – docked one quarter.

'My breeches, woman. My shed breeches.'

'Husband, it's the Sabbath. You don't work on the Lord's Day.'

Jonah climbed back into bed. The Lord's Day. The Sabbath. Day of rest. Sunday best. Clean linen. Church clothes. His breeches airing after Esther's onslaught against the filth of the carotting shed. His mother had shown Esther how to launder them, had passed on her wash-house secrets just as father had once initiated him into the Mysteries of their trade.

'Make the bow sing, young Jonah. Make it sing.'

He could hear it singing in his ears as he fell asleep again.

The fire was lit and Jonah's small clothes warming on the bakestone when Esther heard his cry. She hurried upstairs.

'What is it, Jonah? What's the matter?'

'My head, there's worms crawling in my head.'

'Dearest,' Esther kissed his brow. 'You're not properly rested. Sleep some more now.'

She tidied the bed-covers, turned and plumped the pillow. The motley blotches of stale, blood stained spittle did not surprise her. For many a Monday past she'd started early in the wash-house, secretly soaping Jonah's pillowcase before adding it to the boiling buckwash. But her mother-in-law was not so easily deceived.

'Best save your precious soap. Chamber lye will do as well.'

Esther, stained linen in one hand and soap in the other, began to weep.

'I wanted to spare you the worry.'

'I've worried since he were born,' said Mother Webb, 'but it han't helped none. It's the start. He's going the same way as his father.'

The memory of Old Jonah – dead limbed, toothless, vacant eyed and ranting at things only he could see – terrified Esther.

'No!' she cried. 'I won't let it happen. He'll not go to the shed. I'd rather sleep on the streets.'

But her Jonah would not listen. He meant to finish the work his father had begun. He was so close to getting the better of Briggs, just as Old Jonah had planned. Only then would he leave the carotting shed. Only then would he put down the bow-pin with which he plucked the great bow and walk away from the accursed place.

Jonah fell asleep. Esther put ready his clean clothes. The bed linen could wait till after church.

'We must go together,' insisted Mother Webb. 'Put on your Sunday best. Hold your head up. Smile. Don't give Briggs an inkling.'

The portly Briggs, his wife and entourage proceeded up the aisle to their name-plated pew, their entrance silencing the congregation as might a descent of angels.

Well, Foxy Briggs, thought Mother Webb, your red hair's catching up with the grey wig, but your eye looks just as fiery. We'll get no change out of you. We durst not miss a payment.

Mr. Briggs acknowledged the various bobs and bows of his tenants and employees. He noted the empty places of absentees with decidedly more interest than did the man of God who intoned the litany.

O God the Father of heaven: have mercy upon us miserable sinners.

Samuel Briggs was not miserable. Sing aloud! Praise the Lord! Jonah Webb was not in church. Neither old Mother Webb standing ram-rod straight, nor the fair-faced wife in her best dimity, could fool him. Jonah Webb was sickly. He was succumbing to the felter's fate just like his father. Jonah Webb might not make the final payment. Alleluia!

Esther knelt and prayed her husband might leave the shed. She no longer pleaded for a child. There was no purpose. The worms in Jonah's head had consumed his youth and vigour. He would press his flaggy body against her, moan softly then lapse into a troubled sleep. She despaired at night as she eased herself free from his cold, dank limbs. She despaired every month when he consoled her with the promise that a child would come in God's good time.

Samuel Briggs was a short, barrel-bellied man. Mother Webb suspected he sat on his hassock the better to show off his brocade coat. She watched him bow the knee and make the responses.

That it may please thee to bring into the way of truth all such as have erred, and are deceived;

We beseech thee to hear us, good Lord.

'No, Lord,' prayed Mother Webb. 'Please keep turning a deaf ear. Don't let Mr. High-and-Mighty Briggs know the truth. Don't tell him he's been deceived.'

Foxy Briggs was a big master. Ginger pated and ginger-breaded. Rich enough to buy beaver pelts at the annual spring auction; powerful enough to torch illegal imports and punish any singeing boy who pretended to be skilled. Hats from Samuel Briggs of Southwark were worn in London, Amsterdam and Paris, were shipped to Spain, Portugal and far away to the Americas.

Mother Webb remembered when she and Old Jonah might have sailed to America. There were notices in the news-sheets. Agents paraded the streets of Southwark dishing out handbills and advice for free. Felt-makers were needed in New England. Seven year men who could start up the hatting trade. They could have gone. There was no better felter than her Jonah. Hatters far preferred to finish his hoods than any others. Yes, they could have gone. Offers were made. Offers were pressed. Then Foxy Briggs came running.

'You can't leave me, Jonah, not with trade so good. I forbid it.'

Both men were rising thirty and Jonah the taller and

stronger, but he played the respectful underling to his employer's face.

'You cannot forbid it, sir.'

'But this is your home.'

'But not my house, Mr. Briggs. I pay you rent.'

'They've not offered you a house?' Mr. Briggs was incredulous.

'Oh, they're very anxious to have me,' said Jonah.

'Now, Jonah, don't be foolish. There's an ocean between that promise and its fulfilment.'

'Thank you for the advice, Mr. Briggs. Be assured, if I set my mind on going, I'll serve out my proper notice.'

That it may please thee to preserve all that travel by land or by water ...

Mother Webb thought she might have enjoyed travel, taking ship to a new land. But they were spared the perils of the deep. Mr. Briggs made his offer.

'Do you like this house, Jonah?'

'It's a good, comfortable house, Mr. Briggs.'

'Then your rent henceforth shall purchase it. You remain loyal, Jonah, and this house shall be mortgaged to you. Signed and sealed by a notary.'

Jonah smiled as he shut the door behind his employer.

'Don't look so worried, wife. I know the number of years I need to buy this place and for once, I've got the whip-hand.'

Jonah played his advantage. He talked America with

journeymen already signed to emigrate, took a drink with eager agents and crossed the Bridge to talk passage at the Pool. Mr. Briggs gave in. Jonah got the contract he demanded and the mortgage could pass from father to son.

'But Jonah, we have no son. No child.'

'You're still a fine, strong woman, wife. We will have a son. We must have a son.'

Young Jonah was the light of their lives.

'And the sky is lit to welcome him!' Jonah cradled his firstborn as London celebrated the coronation with torchlight and fireworks. 'God's blessing on the second George, and on the second Jonah Webb.'

The child grew strong and quick-witted, a tall, sturdy limbed youth who followed his father's trade.

'My son is to be bound to the House of Briggs?' cried Mother Webb.

'An indentured man,' said her husband. 'The way I planned for one of us to become a man of property.'

'It might have been easier in America.'

'No, wife. Felt's damn hard work anywhere on earth. And there were no house set aside for us. I just let Briggs think there were.'

Old Jonah guided his apprentice son in the ways of the Worshipful Company of Felt Makers. Seven years and seven Mysteries. First pluck the guard hairs from the beaver pelt. Then make ready each shaft of fur with powder of mercury stirred into good Southwark water. Strip fur from skin and face the hurdle. Play craftsman's music on the hatter's bow and make each fibre dance to your tune.

'Make the bow sing, young Jonah. Make it sing.'

Dance the fibres into one matted batt. Shape six batts into a cone and boil and plank the cone into a hood. Colour with dye, stiffen, stretch and then send to the hatter who has the easy part. The hard work done, he sizes, fashions and sells for good profit.

That it may please thee to defend, and provide for, the fatherless children, and widows …

This was the plea to which Mother Webb made her most fervent response although she knew God to be as deaf as a post. Old Jonah had been dead three years but she was a widow, and her son fatherless, long before he lay in his coffin. The initial signs of the sickness – dribble, bleeding gums, exhaustion – multiplied. His head was in turmoil, his teeth ached, his nose bled. Each morning his limbs had to be rubbed back to life and salve put on his raw, red eye-lids. Slowly, slowly, his churning brain solidified like cream being turned in a butter-tub. He forgot words. He forgot his family. He forgot himself. The numbness creeping over his body could not be rubbed away. His walk became a stagger and he could no longer grasp the bow and make it sing. Young Jonah took his place at the hurdle. The dream of father and son working together to pay Mr. Briggs before time fell by the wayside as Old Jonah's loose teeth fell to the floor.

O God, we have heard with our ears, and our fathers have declared unto us, the noble works that thou didst in their days, and in the old time before them.

Mother Webb argued silently with the minister. The Lord God might have defeated the Pharaoh of Egypt, the prophets of Baal and kings of Babylon, but He seemed powerless against the magic of the beaver people. Those ancient tribes put a curse on stolen pelts, and the combined prayers of every afflicted felt-maker and his family could not remove it.

Favourably with mercy hear our prayers.

Mother Webb gave thanks for one mercy – her son would be spared the worst. They were in the last year of payments and when they had the deeds of the house, Young Jonah could leave the shed. He would be a man of property. The Lord might sit up and listen then.

Fulfil now, O Lord, the desires and petitions of thy servants, as may be most expedient for them …

'Amen,' chanted Esther. 'Amen. Amen.'

But her supplications brought little comfort. The memory of Old Jonah still haunted her as she left the church. She could not answer Mr. Briggs when he enquired after her husband's health. Mother Webb spoke for her and retorted that Jonah was resting as the Lord required of working men having had some experience of six day labour Himself.

But He hasn't any experience of the carotting shed,

thought Esther, and how that labour makes men mad. Mother Webb knew better than the Lord.

'Tell me what'll happen. Every sign. Every symptom. How long before …' Esther faltered. 'I'm afraid, mother, so afraid.'

'Don't be', said Mother Webb. 'Jonah's got time. He'll be out the shed before long.'

'He'd be out tomorrow if I had my way.'

'Then Foxy Briggs would win. He gambled on us running out of time. He'd win and he'd have the house back. It would break Jonah's heart.'

'What about my heart?' cried Esther.

'I was wife to a felter, too.' said Mother Webb. 'I did my share of crying and beseeching the Lord.' She took Esther's hand. 'But sometimes it pays to leave off praying and make your own arrangements. So, my girl, when you want a child more than you want Jonah's child, wipe your eyes, put on your Sunday best and walk over the Bridge to where the sailors come ashore.'

Esther stared at her mother-in-law. The import of her words sank in slowly like a log slung in a Southwark bog.

'But what …' Esther asked at last, 'what if you'd borne a girl child?'

'I'd have put on my Sunday best again,' said Mother Webb.

THE END OF THE PIER

Ten thirty-five Standard Dome Time and we are standing at Methuselah's door. Engineer Redman and I congratulate ourselves. While Mayor Mulhouse was munching doughbars and spitting crumbs all over his desk – Greta has often joked about our leader's eating habits – we have found a witness. But I'm getting ahead of myself, forgetting the rules of journalism. Tell it straight. Start at the beginning.

Like many of my Town Hall scoops, this story owes more to foreplay than forethought. Well, you can't blame a chap when an informant comes as sweetly stacked as Greta. That's a code name – Greta the Grass – I don't know her real name. It helps with tabloid rule number one: never, never reveal the source of information. I stick to that rule religiously. Mind, I do have nightmares that I might buckle if threatened with relocation. Thankfully, MM, that's Mayor 'Mighty' Mulhouse, hasn't twigged yet.

But back to this story. It begins when Greta stops over at my place.

'How's work?' I ask and nibble at her ear.

'Zany!' she says. 'MM's acting real strange.'

I give her an encouraging squeeze.

'How strange?'

'He's throwing doughbars.'

'Throwing doughbars?' I echo.

'Slap bang at the telly,' she says, 'and yelling fit to bust.'

'Something's upset him,' I say as casual as you like and squeeze some more.

Oh, it's real tough scratching stories from the walkways of Barton-by-Sea!

Next morning it's breakfast, a see-you-soon kiss for Greta as she goes off to work, a few chosen words and I'm ready to send in my report.

'Hello, Mac,' says the secretary. 'What's making the news today?'

'Our great leader, of course.'

'Of course! Input now, please.'

'Paragraph one: Rumours that Mayor Mulhouse is slimming can be discounted.' I hear a stifled giggle but continue. 'So can any concern over the quality of doughbars. MM's angry disposal of these delicacies is not a reflection on the ingredients but is occasioned by a telecommercial: ten seconds of musack and the slogan, Bring Spring to Barton-by-Sea.'

'Please explain spring in this context, Mac.'

'It was a season,' I reply. 'Still could be in some domes, I suppose. You ready to continue?'

She murmurs an affirmative.

'An opposition spokesman denied any involvement with the offending advert now showing on the Community Channel. It was suggested that the mayor might be flying a kite.'

I pause.

'Mac?'

'I'm thinking. How about this for an idea? We'll shove in the competition here. Star Prize. Two End of the Pier tickets fly to the reader offering the best explanation of this strange term for testing public opinion.'

'That's one of your better ones, Mac.'

'Thanks, sweetheart. Usual competition layout in bold type. Now, final paragraph: Our leader remains tight-lipped, although it is known that he suspects subversion.'

Mayor Mulhouse is always sounding off about subversion but I decide to check it out as is my habit. I walk the couple of blocks to the T.V. studios and smooth talk information out of a broad in Classified. The spring commercial belongs to an incomer – Engineer Redman. I note his details, kiss my informant and high-tail it over to the Thermal Station where the new boy is employed.

It's easy to pick out Redman. He's the one taking

lunch alone. The residents of Barton-by-Sea have their own way of dealing with upstart incomers.

'Engineer Redman?'

He nods.

'Mind answering a few questions?'

Well, of course he doesn't. There's no better publicity than free publicity.

I sit down and some wise guy in the canteen shouts, 'Watch it, Mac. He might spring at you.'

Redman takes it in good part. He salutes his detractor. 'Success,' he claims. 'Now I know I'm not wasting my money.'

His money? He's funding this advert himself?

'I am,' says Redman.

This guy is not for real. Playing solo! No-one challenges Mayor 'Mighty' Mulhouse on their own.

'Come off it, Redman. What's your angle? Who's behind you?

'No-one,' protests Redman. 'No-one's behind me. I just miss the spring. I didn't think I would, but I do.'

'Your previous dome was programmed for spring?'

'Yes. They held on to seasonal temperatures. The variations made my work more interesting. Spring was my favourite.'

'So why take relocation?' I ask.

'It was promotion. Better pay. Better accommodation. A step up the ladder.' he sighs.

'I thought that's what mattered, but I was wrong. It's the old, old story, isn't it? Waking up when the final whistle's gone.'

'The way of the world, Redman. We can't rewrite history.'

'But we can re-programme the dome,' he urges. 'That's in the constitution. I've checked. If there's enough support, we can bring back spring.'

The man is an innocent. Since when did MM consult the constitution? I've busted a gut for a dreamer with a bad dose of nostalgia. Sorry, Redman. No profitable story here.

I tell Greta about Redman and she turns off the fun stuff. What is it with her tonight? We're having our first quarrel. She begs me to write up Redman's campaign. Waste words on a loser? No way! The man's a joke. A crank. Greta doesn't think so.

'We should ask questions,' she argues, 'query where life is heading before it's too late. If Redman had done that he wouldn't be unhappy, but at least he's asking now.'

What's brought this on? This isn't Barton-by–Sea speak. Where's giddy Greta, my good-time gal?

'MM's going to zap him,' she says. 'Redman needs help.'

'What d'you mean.'

'Find out,' she shouts and flounces out.

The evening falls kinda flat without her. I turn on the telly for company and there's Mayor Mulhouse filling the screen and eye-balling the audience.

'Spring,' he declares, 'will cost you money. A lot of money.'

Holy shit! Call me butter-fingers Mac. The Town Hall is taking Redman very seriously. There is a story with legs and I nearly let it slip. I ring Greta.

'I've been thinking over what you said ...'

'You've been watching telly,' she interrupts.

And before the lie is off my lips, the line goes dead. Now buck up here, Mac. You can't spend time mooning over a broad when there's a story brewing.

'You and his "mightyship" have made the front page again.' The secretary throws me the copy. I read:

SPRING DEBATE HOTS UP

Mayor Mulhouse was at his pugnacious best in the battle of words on spring.

Lone crusader, Redman, seeking support for reprogramming at his first press conference, was no match for Barton's top man.

Redman, who claims experience of spring from his previous placement, extolled the benefits of that forgotten season, but Mayor Mulhouse challenged 'this dubious testimony.' He called the campaigner, 'a lone witness spouting uncorroborated opinion,' and accused the incomer of advocating a backward step.

Our leader warned that converting to a programme of seasonal weather would be a disaster and result in loss of revenue and higher taxes. He concluded to loud applause, 'Redman should do his sums. Success is being a summer dome.'

I tell it like it is. That's my job. Why can't Greta accept that? It's not my fault that MM got the better of the argument. Nobody will want spring if they have to pay for it. But Redman's still campaigning, still smiling – mostly at Greta. I get a strange ache in my gut when she smiles back. I'm jealous. I admit it. She's got to me has Greta. I want us to be together but she's giving me the cold shoulder. This is new to me. I've never had trouble pulling broads before. I'm feeling down. Real miserable.

And then a lifeline drops into my lap. Or rather the secretary drops a sack of mail on my desk. Three cheers for the Fly-a-Kite competition! I'm going through the stack of letters – everyone wants to win a Pier Pass – and there's this letter in spidery old script. He remembers flying a kite. He remembers spring. Jeezez! This is some Methuselah. A real anti-social. But what the heck! He's the winner.

I fall into step with Greta as she leaves work and tell her about Methuselah.

'He might help Redman,' I suggest. 'A proper witness.'

'So old?' she says. 'He can't be genuine, can he?'

Hells bells! Is this what love does? Scrambles the brain. I should have checked it out. People play all sorts of shabby tricks to get a Pier Pass. I cross my fingers and swear that he is. I have an address.

'You've found him?' asks Greta.

'Of course.'

'Mac, you're wonderful.'

'I'm an investigative reporter,' I reply.

Well, it's true. That's how I'm listed. The competitions are just an occasional side-line. A little extra earner for me and the Pier Master. How else would ordinary guys – the likes of Methuselah – get to go on the pier?

'Let's go and tell Redman,' I say and take Greta's hand.

And this is where we came in. Me and Engineer Redman knocking on Methuselah's door. It creaks open. Jeezez! I've never seen anyone so old. This winner is no hoax. Stooped. Shuffling. Silver-haired. A one-off original. I wave the Pier Passes under his nose.

'Mac the News. You wrote me about kites.'

He agrees. He hoped I'd call. He has something for me. But why aren't I alone? Who's my side-kick? He's not agreeing to any photos. Oh, he's all there is this ancient. No ordinary guy. I smell a story. A scoop with a capital 'S'. I introduce Redman.

'The one who wants spring?' asks Methuselah.

'The same.'

He ushers us in.

The place is dilapidated but stuffed with fine furniture. He unlocks a door at the end of a passage and we step into danger. Holy mackerel! There's paintings, photographs, books, files, folders, old DVDs and it's all illegal stuff. I'm ready to back off, but Redman's like a crazy man. Peering. Touching. Reading. Shouting.

'Look, Mac, look … Birds! … Butterflies! Have you ever seen the like? Look … Field-mouse! Seahorse! … Slow-worm!'

'Generation upon generation of my family were naturalists' says Methuselah. 'They recorded so much that was beautiful. I couldn't bear to see their work destroyed and I was right.' His veined hand wipes away a tear. 'It has sustained me over the bleak years of this imprisonment. Others weren't so fortunate.'

I get the picture. A backhander. A hefty backhander. He gets to keep a memory collection and outlives the chancer who took his money. But could there be something in what he says? The elders among initial dome dwellers didn't last long, and now longevity is neither applauded nor desired. I might follow it up, but first things first.

I ask Methuselah about kite flying. Redman scowls but that's our cover. That's what I'm here for – to interview a winner.

'We'd go on the pier,' he recalls. 'Anyone could then. My dad would race me right to the end. Plenty of space there to fly a kite. It was such fun.'

He has an old DVD. A little lad in short pants launching a diamond shaped contraption. He lets it out on a line. It rises and falls and rises again on invisible power. A splash of red with fluttering black tail against a pale blue background.

'Wind power,' explains Methuselah. 'A good windy day could bring tears to the eyes and the kite would nearly tug me into the sky.'

'Way up there,' Redman stabs at the blue, 'is the problem hole.'

Thermal engineers know about these things.

'The Greenhouse Effect,' snorts Methuselah. 'A good name seeing we ended up living in one. Needn't have happened, you know, but no-one wanted to pick up the bill.' He turns to Redman. 'Your spring campaign brought it all back. Same arguments. Same concern with pounds and pence.'

Am I hearing this right? Methuselah doesn't want these Pier Passes. He wants us to have his collection of forbidden memories. He wants it safe before he dies. He knows he hasn't got much time left. I'm thinking double profit instead of a good excuse when Redman lands us right in the proverbial. He grasps the old man's hand. Thanks him. Assures him he's made the right decision. His legacy will be well looked after. Now hold on, Mr. Engineer, hold on. Journalists don't relocate so easy. Mayor Mulhouse will call this subversion. He'll have us suited up and in the paddy-wagon before you can say 'memory collection.'

But Redman doesn't listen. He's gathering up files and folders, photographs, books and DVDs. He's stacking and packing.

'We'll collect after close down,' he says.

'What d' you mean, "we"?' I protest.

'Come on, Mac, use the grey matter. It's safer then. We can be thermal engineers on inspection duty. I'll lend you some gear.'

I can't argue with that and, like Redman reminds me, I've got to look Greta in the eye when we get back. Oh, boy, did I get her wrong, but helping Redman can put things right between us.

We make the pick-up as arranged and bid Methuselah farewell. Redman trolleys the stuff to my place. Holy shit, man! I'm not the guy for this.

'Yes you are, Mr. Journalist,' he argues and Greta agrees.

That's why Methuselah entered the competition. He wanted contact with Mac the News without arousing suspicion. The collection has to be with someone who can use the information it contains. Not immediately perhaps, but one day I must tell Methuselah's story. I must tell the truth of what's been lost. I'm outvoted. But, what the heck, that one day could be a long way off! I'm not going to disappoint my girl now she's back. She thinks I'm a hero and I'm not about to argue. I help unload.

And that's the last time I see Redman. He's not at his place, not at work and the spring advert is withdrawn. I guess he's in MM's mincer. Greta – we both prefer this to her given name – confirms he's been relocated. Labelled, 'Unsuited to summer dome'. Nothing more. No designated placement. No address. Greta's still my grass. Still my girl.

I take my time, let things settle down, before I risk cataloguing Methuselah's legacy. But once I start I cannot stop. I read and note and view. I wonder and wonder at an unknown world – at things like snow, frost, a dragonfly, bumblebee, woodland, hills and rivers. I understand why this stuff is banned. You can miss what you don't know. You can yearn for an Earth that was once abundant and for a life unconfined. And now I'm angry. Why didn't they do something? Stop pollution? Mend the goddam hole? Why didn't they get their act together? But I know the answer. Why didn't Barton-by-Sea want spring?

I watch the old DVD over and over. Young Methuselah flying his kite, flying his kite, flying his kite and I want to go on the pier. I still have the old man's prize in my pocket.

'Right to the end,' I tell Greta and hand in the passes.

We race to the end of the pier and press our noses against the glass. Outside. Land. Sea. Sky. Space to fly a kite. Our lost world. Beautiful. Stunning. Polluted. Poisonous.

'Perhaps one day …' I say and draw Greta close.

I wipe a tear from my cheek and then another. It must be the wind. Don't you know the wind can bring tears to your eyes? Cut the bullshit, Mac. There is no wind in here.